I Bring the Storms

Tell-Tale Publishing's 6th Annual Horror Anthology

2021

Printed in the United States of America

I Bring the Storms
Elizabeth Alsobrooks

Vengeance
Shawn Brink

Friends Don't Let Friends Die Alone
Darren Simon

Hyenas
Rob Tucker

Death by Mummy
Francesca Quarto

Hope You Guess My Name
Ric Wasley

The Intruder
Rob Tucker

As Good as a Blind Man's Candle
Francesca Quarto

The Opal Ring
Elizabeth Alsobrooks

Table of Contents

I Bring the Storms

Elizabeth Alsobrooks

She emerged from the tomb into the sunlight, her hair shining like gilt thread. Up the narrow stone pathway, nearer to where he stood, now deep in shadows as the sun began its descent into the dunes.

His nostrils flared as he sought the floral of her soap mixed so enticingly with the more muted yet pungent and personal sweetness of her pheromone-fueled individual scent. Enticing, though both were currently disguised by spray-on sunscreen and layers of dust-streaked perspiration.

She spent the day moving in and out of the tomb's tight quarters to the torrid confines of the ragged tent jammed with shard-covered tables and satellite-aided archeological equipment. He knew because he'd watched her from a series of computer screens that relied on his own satellites for accurate visual relays. The tent's contents and thus their current progress he evaluated moments ago.

The subject of his rapt attention pushed a hair tie escapee behind her ear and called out to one of the workers, "Ahim, would you please tell father it's nearly dark? He barely touched his lunch. It's time he had a decent meal, but he won't listen to me."

"Sure thing, Ms. Howard," Ahim said with a smile before hurrying down the path toward the dig.

Few men would deny her anything, he thought wryly.

Shouldering a canvas bag, she turned and took the path toward the tent, glancing at the sun. "I've got to set my watch alarm and get him out of there sooner tomorrow," she muttered.

He took a step forward, closer.

"Oh!" She pushed down her surprise with a swallow. He watched the movement of her throat before his attention returned to her eyes. "I-I didn't see you there. Can I help you?"

"Phoenix Ramsey, from the museum. Lady Howard, isn't it?" He extended his right hand.

"Just Layla will do. Nice to meet you, Mr. Ramsey." She glanced down at her hand, scrubbed it against her equally dirty khaki cargo shorts and reached for his hand.

He was surprised by the firmness of that grip, but he was more surprised by her American accent. Although he knew from his staff's research that she had an American mother and went to school there, he also knew she settled permanently with her father in London after her mother's death. "Phoenix will do," he said, smiling.

"Phoenix. Nice to meet you." She returned his smile, her teeth white against the tan of her skin. But what held his attention was not her fine dentistry but the sapphire sparkle of her eyes. They were much more striking in person than in the photographs or digital images he'd seen. "My father-" She turned as the sound of conversation neared the entrance. "Oh, here he comes now."

Not until she called her approaching father to introduce them did he pull his attention from her and extend his hand toward her father. He wasn't interested in the father.

"Ramsey? You're the chairman of the board, aren't you? The chap I owe my thanks for getting me the permit?" He was a man whose physique announced his sense of adventure. Around 6 feet, broad shouldered and lean. There were streaks of gray at his temples but his hair was dark brown otherwise. She had her father's smile. Though he had deep creases running from the edges of his lips into his beard, they seemed only to emphasize how often and easily his lips turned upward. His tone was cheerful and amiable. He trusted too easily.

"Think nothing of it. I came to introduce myself and invite you to dinner. I would have done so sooner, but I have been in Italy on business the last few weeks."

"Very good of you. Appreciate it. Dinner? Tonight? Could do with a good meal, or so my daughter keeps reminding me." His arm reached to rest easily across her shoulders and give her an affectionate squeeze. "You're much younger than I imagined, someone with your business holdings and successes. Handsome chap. Gads, even taller than me. All that dark hair and regal bearing. Surprised you're not married."

Phoenix noted the elbow Layla dug into his side and chuckled. "Always busy. No time to meet the right woman, I suppose. Glad you can attend. I shall send a car around to your hotel. Is 7 an appropriate time? Does that give you enough time to get back and rinse the day's hard work off?"

"You're too kind. Plenty of time. See you this evening then."

Nodding, Phoenix said, "I look forward to it," turned and hurried to the car. The sun had lowered but still felt brutal despite his hat and shades. His driver opened the back door and he slipped into the cool interior and reached for his phone.

"Did you get it?" His assistant affirmed his acquisition and Phoenix smiled. "Just in time," he murmured.

****

"You have one of the most impressive collection of antiquities I've seen outside a museum," said the Earl. "I never get tired of seeing it."

"Coming from you, a compliment indeed, My Lord."

"Now what must I do to get you to drop the honorifics, Phoenix. Please, call me Archie. I feel like we are chums after the past few months. Who else has a billiards table around here? And after the strings you pulled to get a permit in a matter of weeks that would have taken me years I am forever in your debt."

"No need for thanks. I was right about you. You have uncovered a wealth of information and helped add merit to the theory that Narmer depicted as a warrior king was just custom, and the kingdom along the Ar was peaceful at that time."

"There, you see? What other layperson would refer to the Nile as Ar? You should have been an archaeologist, Phoenix. You know as much about ancient Egypt as I. Sometimes you speak as if you lived it."

"You are too kind. An enthusiastic hobbyist at best. I inherited both the seat on the museum board and my father's desire to keep our antiquities in Egypt."

"Phoenix, is this new?" Layla called.

"No, quite old really." He turned to the Earl. "Shall we?" he asked, gesturing across the room.

The two men crossed between glassed and well-lit displays of ancient pottery, hieroglyphic covered tablet fragments and even an intricately carved sarcophagus that bore the remnants of what was once brightly colored paint. They stopped beside Layla who still gazed upon a life-size painting of a figure that if one judged by his apparel appeared to be a pharaoh.

"Is this you? Minus the beard here of course. Why would you have a painting done of you in that clothing?" Layla asked.

"I just had it restored. It's hundreds of years old, and what the artist imagined as the first pharaoh from the 0 dynasty. It has no real value as it's from a little known artist, but I thought it was interesting."

"What's most interesting is that it actually looks like you. The fact that some artist painted it hundreds of years before you were born is uncanny," said the Earl.

"I didn't see it at first, but the friend I was with in a dusty little antiquities shop insisted on buying it for me, as a joke. I thought it was funny, a bit of a conversations piece. I only just ran across it recently in the back of a closet and had it restored. The colors are quite vibrant."

"They're amazing. At first I thought perhaps it was one of those things they do like caricatures that make you look like someone else, but you don't seem at all the type."

"Now that it's been restored I have to admit that even I can see a resemblance, so it is indeed surprising. I don't really want to look at it every day, which is why I had it installed on a side wall at the end of the collection gallery, to be found as you did today by guests examining the artifacts."

"Well, you are Egyptian and rumored to be as wealthy as a pharaoh," the Earl responded with a deep chuckle.

"I'm surprised the artist wasn't well know. The painting is in and of itself quite masterfully done," Layla said, tilting her head to peer at the small, scrawled signature. "Does that say Kent? Can't make out the surname."

"It might. We're not sure either. I actually had someone look into finding other work by this artist but we have yet to turn up anything," Phoenix said.

"Hm. Very curious," Layla said softly.

***

It wasn't the only thing she thought a little off while she sat on her balcony the next morning with a milk tea in one hand and her cell phone in the other. She hoped Viv could help her sort out her feelings.

"He's intriguing, Vivian." She took a sip of the acidic brew and said, "Of course I love him. I just can't believe how much in such a short amount of time. It's only been four months."

She put her phone down, pressed the speaker button, and shoved bangs not quite grown out behind her ear.

"I thought you told me you felt absolutely exhilarated every time he was going to pick you up for a date. When's the last time you felt that way about a man?" Layla could imagine Vivian, hands on hip, her brow furrowed in aggravation. Viv made a great college roommate, but sometimes acted more like a scolding mother. Instead of commiserating, she was challenging Layla's confusion. "I wish I felt that way about a man ever! The man is one of the best catches in the world, Layla. He loves you. You love him. What's the problem? Did he shove a 1200 pages prenup in your face or a 5 carat flawless emerald on your finger?"

"Vivian, must you be so vulgar? I wouldn't be a gold digger even if I needed to be." She lifted the cup to her mouth and took a few swallows of the cooling liquid. Vivian was impossible to argue with. She made up her mind about something and wasn't easily swayed.

"I know you're not, but I'm just pointing out that the man is perfect for you, and that's what seems to bother you. I just don't get it. Cold feet?"

Vivian was making sense. "Maybe. I think you might be right. I'm just waiting for that fatal flaw to show up." Layla sighed. "It's almost as if I'm afraid of my own feelings. I mean, I am so completely besotted by him I'm afraid something will go wrong."

"So marry him before it does." Vivian, always the optimist, Layla thought. "Once you're married you can work through any difficulties as a couple. He's handsome, broad-shouldered and a head taller than you when you're in heels, every woman's dream, Layla. I about had a heart attack when you texted me that photo. But when I saw him on that news program where he gave a statement about some merger or other, the man has the bearing of, of a pharaoh!"

Layla broke out laughing. "I'll have to text you a photo of the painting he has at his place sometime. All the suave confidence and well-mannered breeding comes from his international business dealings and generations of the best schooling money can buy. Now that's a legit thing since you brought it up, Vivian. How much time do you think he'll actually spend with me? We haven't even discussed if he wants or expects me to jet set with him. I like to travel, but I also like kicking around inside old dusty tombs with my father."

"Details, luv. You need to figure out what's really making you hesitate. Look, no matter what, you are the one who has to decide. Just follow your heart. It won't steer you wrong."

"That's the problem. My head and my heart are at war. Before you say it, I know, I know, I always overthink things. Listen, thanks, Viv. You always know how to get me thinking more clearly. Now I need to just be honest with myself."

"Don't worry about what others will say or think, and I know that's in the back of that noggin of yours. Call me once you decide. Love you."

"You, too. Bye-bye." Layla slid the red button and pushed her fingers through her hair. The slight breeze blew it into her face and she tucked it behind her ears. She wished Vivian wasn't so far away in America. A glance at her watch told her the statuesque female was probably coiffed to the nines and sitting behind her glass desk working, while still finding time to talk to her confused friend half a world away. Viv was always so clear headed and made snap decisions with ease.

Maybe Viv's right. Maybe I am worried that Phoenix is too perfect, too good to be true. Everyone knows if something or someone is too good to be true . . . they're fake.

So what could he be hiding?

The night before she noticed that he rarely did more than push his food around his plate. He didn't seem to like anything but meat, and that he ate so bloody raw she kept her attention averted elsewhere until the plate was taken away. It must be safe and prepared correctly. She'd never had a meal with him that didn't deserve at least 2 if not 3 Michelin Stars. They'd never uncorked a bottle of wine that wasn't even to her rather refined taste, superb. Perhaps she was trying to find fault because she sometimes felt unworthy of his intense devotion and love. Whenever they were together he made her feel like she was the only important person in the world.

Perhaps the fact that she realized she was unconditionally in love with him frightened her. She'd never been in a relationship this serious before.

He always made her laugh and did unexpected things like taking her horseback riding along the Nile and riding dune buggies in the desert at night under the stars. He even, much to her shock, convinced her to hand glide off a pyramid. Who knew how he got permission for that. She lifted her left hand and stared. Last night he'd taken her in a hot air balloon and asked her to marry him and given her this enormous princess cut emerald surrounded by diamonds engagement ring to help her think it over as they drifted above the valley of the kings.

She hadn't given him an answer yet.

She'd only been dating him for four months. She must be crazy. It was even crazier that her father, her conservative, over-protective father thought that it was a great idea.

Of course Viv agreed with him and knew a lot more gritty details than her father, like how he looked even better without his clothes and was the most amazing lover Layla had ever had. She couldn't even think when they were together, but what she felt was mind-blowing.

The plus side kept getting longer. And there was the fact that he told her he had a penthouse in New York and a mansion in London among other places, here being one, Italy, she couldn't remember where all he'd said, but the New York and London residences were meant to reassure her that she'd be close to friends and family on whatever continent she desired. She understood why he was so good at business negotiations; he asked questions for which he took great pains to predetermine the answers.

Well, if the only reason she could think of to say no was that she hadn't known him long enough, the logical answer was yes. With her decision made, Layla finished her tea and pushed away from the table to go meet her father. He was going to have a very good day.

When Phoenix returned from Italy in two days, he would be pleased too.

****

"Miss me?"

Layla shielded her eyes from the blowing sands, but she didn't need to see to recognize his voice. "Always." The wind picked up and sand blasted against her face. "Oh!"

Phoenix quickly lifted his arm and used the sleeve of his kaftan to shield her, leading her back down the path and into the tomb. "It is a good thing your father asked me to see what was keeping you. The storm is full upon us now."

"I would have been on my way, but I left my phone in the tomb. I was taking some photos earlier. I was going to send them to you. Did father tell you we cleared the far wall today?"

"He did mention that. Your phone could have waited, my dear. Were you not worried about being stuck here in the middle of a sandstorm?"

"Yes, but I thought I had enough time. It was foolish. I'm glad you came." She lowered her voice as they moved into the antechamber. The noise from the storm subsided. "Come here. Now I can show you in person." She pointed toward some hieroglyphs on the far wall and headed toward them.

"You cleaned the entire wall today?" he asked.

"No, it took us a couple days, but several of the crew members helped. We were anxious to decipher it. We're not positive what this means, because we doubt they were actually blood drinkers, but it sure looks like they had some sort of vampire folklore."

"Though uncommon, it has been found in other funerary murals. It is thought to depict eternal life, is it not?" Phoenix said softly.

"Yes, but I don't think I've seen anything quite this graphic before. The last one I saw had a goblet with several droplets of what might have been blood above it. This one has what looks like a servant with their neck cut open, and a noble person holding a cup to catch the blood flowing from the open wound."

"That is much different. What about this," Phoenix said, rubbing the dust away from a hieroglyphic and then pressing another symbol."

There was a labored grating sound of sand ground between stone and the wall quivered. Layla gasped and stepped away. As they watched, a section of the wall slid outward. "Phoenix, did you know that was there?"

"Happy accident. The way many wondrous discoveries are made."

"We need to see what's in there." Layla grabbed a lantern off the floor and headed through the doorway.

Grabbing her arm, Phoenix said, "Hold up, love. I will go first. You never know what you may find. Traps are common."

"It's fine. I'll be careful. I have more first-hand experience," she said and continued through the opening.

Phoenix grabbed a torch from a wall sconce and followed. Once inside a much larger and vaulted chamber, he reached his hand behind him, and lit another torch hanging on the wall.

"How did you know that was there?" Layla asked, turning to watch as he moved around the chamber lighting other torches. "Them. How did you know any of those were here?"

He shrugged, continuing along the wall. "They were in the antechamber, so it seemed reasonable that they would be here. Move no further. Do you see the images on the wall? There are slits in the side walls, and likely triggers in the floor that will release some sort of deterrent against thieves. It's a common technique from this era."

"You're right. I see them."

As he walked back, he reached down to pick up rock fragments. He slammed them with force in front of him and scattered them across the stone floor.

An instant response sent wooden darts flying from slits on both side walls. "Stay behind me. I don't care how much experience you have, I am a lot bigger and can survive a poison dart much more readily than you." He didn't pause for her to argue but moved forward and repeated the procedure three more times until he nearly crossed the room. Then he walked to light torches on the side walls.

"Oh my!" Layla cried out. "Look at all the gold! That's gold. It's got to be gold. Who was buried here? Look at the sarcophagus. It's actually undamaged. I don't think this tomb has ever been disturbed. The statuary and the—this is incredible! This is the find of a lifetime!"

"You and your father's expedition will get all the credit, my dear. But do you think we should try to secure it and let your father in on the discovery? It will all need to be catalogued."

"Oh, you're right. I know you're right. He will be so disappointed if he doesn't get to explore further. And look, there's an opening behind that sarcophagus. Do you think there's another room beyond it?"

"It looks likely. We should let your father discover that. I know it makes you want to explore until you collapse on the floor from exhaustion, but I think the storm has passed and your father is probably frantic with worry."

Layla sighed. "I know you're right, but this is so exciting! Hold on one second." She stepped back and aimed her phone camera at the far wall and flashed away. Then she grabbed Phoenix by the hand and began dancing around, laughing. Her eyes sparkled with delight. "Come on," she said, reaching on tip-toe to kiss him soundly on the mouth. "I can't wait to tell my father!" Then she all but dragged him from the chamber, nearly running in her exuberance.

***

"Have you forgiven me at last? That was a long time to be angry, even for you, Ramsey."

He studied the beautiful blond standing just inside his office. She was dressed in the highest fashion, rubies, her favorite, dangling from her earlobes. He once found her amusing. Now he felt little more than boredom. "I decided to give you a chance to redeem yourself. I have not yet decided whether I will forgive you yet. Did you leave the mummy I had Ahmed procure in that sarcophagus?"

"Alex helped me."

"You look much better than when Alex and Raul went to fetch you. They sent me a photo."

"They gave me the best bottle I ever drank."

"I'm sure you were quite thirsty. Let us hope you learned an important lesson, Calea."

"It is not one I shall ever forget, I promise."

"I see you have replenished your wardrobe with Mosha's help."

"I have most happily replaced my tattered clothing. This fabric is so much more comfortable, and I still get to drape myself in pretty jewelry. Mosha said it's called bling."

"Yes, credit cards are convenient. So are private planes. If you leave first thing in the morning, you will arrive in Spain by lunchtime, and you know what I expect you to do. Begin tomorrow afternoon as the new board chair and interrogate the company executives. Rachel will act as your executive secretary and give you whatever assistance you need."

"I promise I will not let you down. How shall I keep the others from finding out what I am up to?"

"Persuade them not to consult each other. You still remember how?" She nodded. "I want to know who is embezzling and how widespread the corruption is. What other companies or their executives are in on it? Get ahold of me as soon as you know and do nothing about it until I give you directions. I am sending a security team with you. This is a chance to gain my forgiveness. If you betray me again, I will end you."

"I am so sorry. I will earn your trust again." Her tone was pleading but not desperate. She must think he cared about her. "I was jealous and foolish. I never meant to kill her, but just to scare her away."

He frowned. Had he been too lenient? "Sending you away will help you keep your promises," Phoenix said, motioning for her to leave. Rachel and Calea bowed and left the room.

***

Layla felt exhausted but too excited to sleep. She sat down at the desk and downloaded her camera photos to her laptop and enlarged the first photo, deciphering the hieroglyphics before she jotted the translations down in her notebook.

She reached for a cup of herbal tea the bellhop just delivered, her attempt to calm herself enough to sleep. A sound came from the balcony and she glanced up. The sheer drapery billowed on the balcony doors, open to catch the cool evening breeze. Satisfied, she returned to her work.

Another sound snapped her attention back.

"What? Who are you?" Layla jumped from her chair and took an instinctive step away from the now wide open doors.

"A better question is who in hades are you? It's not possible. You can't be alive."

Who was this woman dressed in a flowing red dress with equally scarlet lipstick that contrasted starkly with the dark knoll around her eyes. "Why shouldn't I be alive?"

"Because, my dear," the strange woman said, moving into the room, "I killed you."

Layla backed toward the door to the sitting room. *Can I get there before this lunatic reaches me?* she wondered. She turned to run and glanced back over her shoulder. *Did someone just grab crazy lady and pull her through the doors?* The curtains billowed outward. Her direction changed and Layla ran toward the balcony. She slammed the doors and threw the latch. Her hand pushed back the curtain and she peered out at a now empty terrace. *What just happened? Who are they? What do they want? And how did they get up here on the second floor anyway?*

This time she ran out the door and across the sitting room that connected her hotel suite to her father's calling, "Father! Father!"

***

Phoenix bent down to meet her upturned lips and accepted her response. Now, as always, she melted into his arms. He ignited passion within her from a single caress, even a momentary kiss. Whenever she was with him, her doubts fell away. This time it was her fear. She never before realized how safe he made her feel, how protected.

He raised his head and said, "You were trembling. Are you still afraid? The woman and her accomplice were captured and will never try to rob anyone again. I promise. Even so, I have guards outside the hotel under your balcony, in the hallway outside your suite."

"I'm fine, now that you're here."

"Let me speak to your father. There is a little house near my own that I will rent for you. I thought it would be more convenient for you here, with the room service and restaurants, but if you move into that house, I will make sure it's fully staffed with security, a housekeeper and a chef."

"That's not necessary, Phoenix. I'll be fine, really."

"Or you could say yes, have a small intimate wedding and leave for our honeymoon." He smiled down at her and chuckled. "You do want to tell me yes, right?"

She didn't resist a moment longer, but said simply, "Yes."

"Really?" She nodded and he smiled as he wrapped his arms around her. "I know you still have things you want to discuss with me, such as if I expect you to travel with me on business, if you'll still be able to do what you love and work with your father, or—"

"How could you know exactly what I was wondering?"

"My most important job is to know and understand you so that I can make you happy as well as safe. You are happy; you won't regret saying yes, will you? You didn't say it just because I make you feel safe?"

Layla pulled away and grasped his hands. "No, I most definitely did not say yes because your presence makes me feel safe."

He made her feel safe because she loved and trusted him. He was incredibly strong, so in control. If that isn't attractive enough, he was so masculine with that firm jaw and the way his hair defied its precise styling and fell across his forehead but didn't dare get in his eyes. Ever. When he took her in his arms she could feel his hard, muscled abs, but she have no idea when he found time to work out. Layla pulled away. What was she just thinking about? It felt like she was about to do or say something, and then just forgot.

"Here you are, you two." The Earl walked toward them from the elevator.

"Father. You-you're here. We were, we were waiting for you to go into breakfast, father," Layla said. What had she been about to say? Why did she suddenly feel confused?

"I suppose we have time for one of those tasty meat on dough things and a coffee with plenty of sugar. Then we must hurry to the site."

***

"I didn't touch her! I just wanted to see for myself. Rachel told me she looked just like—" Calea didn't finish. She gasped. Gasped again.

Then ceased.

The body made a soft thump when it fell to the thick Persian carpet.

Her skin darkened and turned gray, the transformation moving outward from where the dagger protruding from her chest. Desiccated flesh shrank around protruding veins blackened by coagulation.

"This is why I don't give second chances to murderous traitors. Get rid of this," Phoenix said, pointing at the body.

His personal bodyguard and indispensable right-hand, Alex, pressed his earpiece and murmured softly. A moment later the door opened and two large men hurried into the room carrying a tarp as if they'd been expecting the order. They laid it down, lifted the body onto it, wrapped it and carried it from the room. Alex closed the door behind them and stood before it, hands clasped in front of him.

"Ask Rachel to come in," Phoenix said, sitting down at his desk.

Soon an attractive petite brunette entered wearing a tailored black business suit with gold double-breast buttons fastened with fine chains. Her four-inch stilettos click-clacked across the wooden floor until she reached the carpet. She stopped in front of the desk.

"Why did you tell Calea about Layla?"

"A test, to see if she was really sorry for killing Neelai or still irrationally jealous. You told me to watch her, and as you know I never thought you should forgive or release her. I didn't trust her."

"She had no reason to hate Layla. Layla is not Neelai."

"She's the doppelganger. She has to be. There was no time limit or acceleration."

"I should have been more specific in my orders."

Rachel shrugged. "Perhaps. You staked Calea as soon as she killed Neelai, so she didn't know that ceremony ever happened. She wouldn't know the difference. She didn't in fact. Calea thought Layla was Neelai. But I grabbed her and swept her away before Layla knew what happened. All Layla was left with was confusion. I assumed you would clear that up."

"She and her father think it was thieves, and that you were a man. They've been relocated to the safe house."

"I hope you understand why I told Calea about Layla."

He couldn't stop his displeasure or the frown it produced, but he had lived long enough to remain silent and keep his anger in check.

Rachel studied his face and he saw her tense, but she continued. "She felt betrayed when you abandoned her for Neelai. It wasn't until then that she believed what you had always told her, that you didn't love her. Jealousy is a powerful emotion. I saw her despair and desperation first-hand, and warned you she wouldn't let it go, even after all this time. The hatred and rage on her face when she thought Neelai had survived the poisoned dagger she--"

His control snapped and he threw the paperweight from his desk so hard it flew through the wood paneling and they heard it shatter onto the marble in the hallway. When he spoke, he modulated his tone to help remove the fear that shone in Rachel's eyes. "I'm afraid you will have to go to Spain without Calea's help. Or, if you feel it necessary I can have Victor fly in from Italy to accompany you."

"No, no, that won't be necessary, your highness. I'm happy to go with just the security crew."

"Good. Once you get there and assess the situation, call immediately if you need more help."

"I will. We'll leave now. The jet is waiting."

He nodded and wondered if her hurry from the room was an eagerness to set off for her task or to escape his presence.

Alex pressed his earpiece and gave directions about wall repair. Then he walked toward the desk and said, "Will you be needing the car this evening?"

***

The waiter filled Layla's wine glass and disappeared into the shadows of the dimly lit restaurant. Phoenix didn't like distractions and was a frequent enough patron for the server to know.

"I haven't seen your personal assistant in a while, Phoenix," Layla commented. "She usually whispers information in your ear at least once in a while. Is she on vacation?"

"She's in Spain on business. Why the sudden interest?"

"Just curious as to why Alex called to tell me the florist wanted me to stop by and give final approval on the flowers, and why he's your only hovering companion these days, except for the security detail, of course. And while I'm speaking of security details, do you think you could call mine off? I'm picking up my best friend, Vivian, who is flying in from America for the wedding tomorrow. I know we're keeping it small, but I had to invite my best friend."

"As you should. But if your friend is coming, it's all the more reason to keep both you and your friend safe, my love."

Phoenix had the firm no discussion tone in his voice that he used when talking business on the phone or giving directives to his staff. He seldom used it with her, but whenever he did, she immediately felt she should do as he asked. Sometimes, later, she wondered why she agreed to his opinions so easily, but quickly dismissed the notion. He requested her opinion on everything from cake flavors and design to anything she wanted changed in the home they would share after their marriage.

Rather than argue, she explained that, "It's just so embarrassing. What will I tell her?"

"Try telling her the truth, that your fiancé has made a few enemies over the years, because business on the scale of investment money I deal with causes some pretty cutthroat competition. People can be very sore losers. And because you--"

"Because I'm important to you, someone might try to harm or kidnap and ransom me."

"Exactly, my dear. Are you ready to order?"

Layla looked down at the menu and said, "Almost. I can't decide between the prawn and the lamb, or perhaps . . . let me just take another look. I haven't eaten here before. What do you suggest?"

Phoenix signaled the waiter and said, "We'd like a buffet. Bring us one of all your dishes so we can sample them."

"Right away, sir," the waiter said before rushing away to place their order.

"That's so extravagant, Phoenix, but I can't lie and say it isn't a fun and enticing idea. Will we be getting one of all the desserts too? Aren't you worried I'll get fat?"

He laughed and said, "What's the sense of having money if I can't indulge the woman I love?"

"You'll spoil me," Layla said.

"It makes me happy to do so, which means you should humor me and allow it, love." He leaned forward and smiled; his gaze so intense she felt he could see into her soul. It startled her for a moment, but then she felt such an overwhelming surge of love and adoration everything else, even the room, seemed to melt away.

"Be sure when you see your friend that you reassure her you have no second thoughts or misgivings about me or the wedding, Layla. I would be so disappointed if she didn't like me or think that we make a wonderful couple."

"No-no I would never let Vivian think we're not the perfect match, Phoenix," she said, and then felt worried that anyone wouldn't see what a sweet and loving husband Phoenix was going to make.

***

"It's great to see you and I do want to catch up, but I'm so exhausted, Layla," Vivian said as they walked down the hallway. "I couldn't get to sleep on the plane, and there's only so many games you can play on your notepad or movies you can watch on a 10 hour flight. Thank goodness I was able to book a nonstop. I still don't know how those people in coach survived. If I couldn't have reclined in my own little nookie, I would have gone nuts."

"Oh, of course you must be exhausted. Take a multivitamin and drink some bottled water before you have a nice tub soak and then sleep as long as you need. This little house Phoenix found us is very quiet. There's hardly any traffic on the street outside." She pointed out the window on the landing. "The wedding isn't for 3 weeks but when you are up to it, I want to take you shopping. They have beautiful clothes here and you can find something smashing that befits the maid of honor. They even have tailors that can do alterations practically while you wait."

Vivian gave Layla a hug. "You look wonderful. You look so happy, too, which makes me happy. I can't wait, and as soon as I get myself over this jetlag, I'll fulfill my duties as maid of honor perfectly."

"I know you will," Layla said, laughing and pointing to the door they now stood before. "Here's your room. Your luggage is inside, and there's plenty of beverages in the mini fridge. There's fruit and snacks on the side table too. If you want something more substantial, just let me know."

***

"So when do I get to meet this American beauty whose praises you have sung so convincingly?" Phoenix asked, taking a swallow from his coffee cup.

"She'll be down shortly. She slept 14 hours but said she's still a little tired. Couldn't sleep on the plane."

"You should have suggested she take a sleeping pill. It's the only way to survive those flights."

"You're right. It's what I do on anything over 7 hours and especially when I leave at night." They both glanced toward the stairway. "Oh, here comes our sleeping beauty now."

Phoenix rose as Vivian approached the breakfast table.

"You're even better looking in person," Vivian said, holding out her hand.

Phoenix grasped it and turned it palm down, kissing the top. "Very nice to meet the woman who is so dear to my beloved. She was not exaggerating about your beauty, either. You could be an Egyptian queen."

"And charming too. No wonder Layla is so smitten with you," Vivian said, smiling. She glanced at Layla and added, "You're lucky you found him first, girlfriend."

As Vivian sat down and accepted the cup of coffee the maid handed her, Phoenix studied her face. She reminded him of a beautiful Nubian priestess he had as a lover over two thousand years ago. She had the same flawless caramel skin, long lean figure and graceful bearing. Even the rows of braids decorated with colorful threads were similar to those worn by Rahela, though hers had been adorned with pure gold beads and a gold serpent that encircled her head, its fanged head protecting her forehead. He needed to introduce Vivian to Alex. If they became a couple, Layla's best friend could be her companion for eternity.

***

Layla's hand shook as she lifted the lid on the urn. Ash. That's all that was left of a man who had been so alive, so energetic just a few weeks ago. She shook the jar and scattered her father's ashes across the side of the tomb. Let her father rest with the royalty he admired most. She sobbed, heartbroken. Phoenix put his arms around her, and she felt comforted.

She glanced up and he said softly, "All will be well, my love," and she believed him.

***

Vivian released her newest shopping bag to the outstretched hand of a bodyguard and smiled her thanks.

"I could get used to this, Layla," she said, laughing. "Hon, I'm so glad I'm on summer break and could be here for you, but if you need me to, I can take a sabbatical and stay longer. There are plenty of history grad students looking for extra teaching income."

"You don't need to do that for me, Vivian. I have Phoenix and we've decided not to postpone the wedding any longer. Father would have wanted me to go on with my life."

"That's wonderful, Layla. I agree your father would want you to go ahead with the wedding. I wouldn't miss it for the world. To be honest, I have been thinking about transferring to the university in Cairo."

"What? Since when? Why?" She turned to look at her friend who she thought told her everything.

"Well, not only does my best friend live here, but Alex has asked me to marry him."

"Are you serious? But you've only known him for a couple months! I knew you were dating, and I knew you liked him, but marriage?

Already?" That explained why Viv had been unavailable lately, why she hadn't been there for her when she needed to talk. Alex.

"I seem to recall a similar conversation last spring."

Layla forced a small laugh. "Well, what was your response to his question?" she said and tried to keep the anxious tone out of her voice.

"I told him I wanted to talk to you first. I know you've poured yourself into your work to help you deal with your father's death so I wasn't sure how you'd react."

At least Viv noticed that. "It's true that I've had a hard time becoming an orphan. I mean, my mom was sick with cancer for several years so even though I was heartbroken, I knew it was coming. But my father was only 45 years old. He never had any heart problems before, so I still don't understand how he had a heart attack. Ahim said he tried to revive him, but he just didn't respond and they were thirty minutes from the nearest medical center." Now she sounded pathetic. She knew her father's death was a tragedy, but she was feeling much better about it. Phoenix told her just last night their future was going to be filled with happiness. He never lied to her.

"Did you ever figure out what urgent message he had for you? He said he discovered the key to deciphering the wall. Did you find it?"

That's right. Why had she forgotten about that? They passed by a bridal shop and Layla said, "No, if only I had been with him that day, but I had a wedding dress fitting and needed to taste cakes and things that seem stupid when I think that if I had been there, I might have . . . I don't know, done something."

Vivian slipped her hand under Layla's arm. "There's nothing you could have done and those things were not stupid." They stepped off the curb to cross the street.

Layla felt herself lifted in the air and forcefully pulled back from the street. She inhaled and turned her head when she heard Vivian yelp.

"What the hell?" Vivian said.

A car sped past, a car that would have struck them as they ventured into its pathway.

Layla grabbed Vivian's arm. She felt her trembling. "Oh! We could have been killed!" Omar released her and she hugged Vivian. "Thank you," she said, glancing back at Omar and Hamid. "Thank you."

"Yes, yes, thank you. We should have been paying attention," Vivian added, hugging Layla back.

Layla's security team just nodded and stepped away. Layla turned back to Vivian and said, "About your earlier question. Life is too short. There are no guarantees. Look, if it makes you happy to marry Alex, I support whatever you decide. I really like Alex. He's funny and kind and very handsome with those thick curls, I might add."

***

"Why did you want to come to the dig site the night before our wedding, Phoenix? Even I haven't been here for two days since those horrible storms have prevented traveling across the desert."

"Sandstorms can be treacherous even in the modern era. The sand clogs engines and can leave vehicles stranded. Without protection they can flay the flesh off man or beast."

"Yes, we are always very careful about staying out of the desert when there's such terrible sandstorms. But it's funny, the weather reports didn't predict them, and they even said they were uncertain where they came from or why they lasted so long. Or why they were only in the desert but not in the city. Then, suddenly you say you want to show me something and they just end, just like that. Even the weather bends to your will, it seems." Layla laughed and grasped his hand, leading him down the pathway to the tomb's entrance.

"I was going to wait and tell you after the wedding, but when Alex told me you and Vivian were chatting and would have been struck by a vehicle this morning if the security team hadn't grabbed you and pulled you out of the street at the last moment, I wasn't willing to chance losing you again."

"Losing me again?" She stopped and looked up at him, puzzled.

He didn't explain but instead tugged on her hand and she followed him into the tomb. Grabbing a torch, he took his hand from hers and reached into his pocket for a lighter.

"I have a flashlight on a bench over here," she said. "Or if you want me to go start the generator we have lights strung across the first two chambers."

He lit the torch.

"Okay, firelight it is. What was so important that you wanted to come here so late in the afternoon?" she asked.

"This way," he said, crossing the room and lighting the torches along the way. He continued through the far chamber and when they reached the wall she and her father had not yet finished deciphering, he placed his hand, palm down, upon a symbol on the wall that neither she nor her father had ever seen before.

As before, the wall began to move. It grated and opened with a soft swoosh of stale air escaping from a space in which it had been confined for a millennium.

"There's another chamber? But how did you know? What is that fragrance? It smells like flowers."

He didn't answer, but instead continued into the crypt and reached to light a torch in a wall sconce he seemed to know would be there. Then he walked around the room and lit more torches until the room became fully illuminated.

Layla walked forward a few steps, then stood and stared. The stone room was filled with gold and bejeweled statuary and jewelry. There was even a brightly painted chariot being pulled by a golden stallion, a throne, and baskets of what Layla knew would later be identified as figs and barley and fruits. But amid the amazing display, what drew her attention was the gossamer clothed body of a woman who appeared to float above an intricately carved golden slab that resembled an altar of some kind.

"What the hell, Phoenix?" She shuffled forward a few feet, her hand reaching out to touch the horse, assuring herself it was indeed real. As if against her will, she felt drawn to the figure at the far end of the room. When at last she stood before it, she sucked in a deep breath and breathed in and out again, realizing she'd been holding it.

"Oh my God," she said softly. She looked around for Phoenix and discovered him standing on the other side of the altar. He watched her intently, his expression serious, almost anxious. "Who is this, Phoenix?"

"Who do you think it might be?" he said, and this time she heard the tension in his voice.

"It might, I mean, I don't know. It looks like my twin sister."

"Not your twin. Neelai. I had my priests cast a spell over Neelai's body over one thousand years ago, and now after all these years . . . We didn't think it worked because Neelai wasn't resurrected then and there. But apparently it did work, just not as we expected, and not then, not until now. When Rachel saw you with your friend in that fashion magazine, she knew immediately who you were."

"I don't understand. Who do you think I am? What are you talking about?"

"Do you know what a doppelganger is? You were conjured by my priests a millennium ago. This was you, and I have waited for you to return for a long, long time, Layla."

Layla frowned. Did she already know this? It seemed familiar, like she had already been told. "I'm not sure . . . you waited for me, or waited for her? She looks like she's alive." Layla reached out to touch the female who appeared to be asleep, but an invisible barrier prevented any contact. She pressed her hands against it, but though she didn't see anything it was like pressing her hands against a glass wall.

"My wife, my queen, Neelia. She is dead, murdered with a magically poisoned dagger."

"Your queen? A thousand years ago? What? Magic? There is no such queen in all of Egyptian history. And why does she look as if she's just sleeping if as you claim she's that old?"

"Not all history as you of all people should realize is known or recorded. As to her preservation, call it science or call it magic, but I had my priests preserve her. She did not deserve to die simply because she loved me, and she certainly did not deserve to have her beauty fade and turn to dust."

"Your priests? You keep talking about your priests. Who are you? Science? There is no such science, or magic! And what of you?"

"Come here."

Layla wanted to run away, willed herself to flee, but found herself hurrying around the altar. Phoenix grasped her hand and pressed it against his chest. She could feel his heartbeat, strong and steady. "How old are you?" Was she dreaming? None of this could be real. What was happening? Her own heart thundered beneath her ribs. A scream lodged in her throat and she swallowed it down so she could breath. She loved him so much. How could he have lied to her? Did he even love her? She sniffed, her eyes filling with tears.

"As old as you fear and more," he said softly, his hand clasping hers firmly. "But I am real, and I do love you. You are not dreaming."

"Ha-how . . . *can you read my mind? How do you always know what I'm thinking?*"

"Yes."

Said so matter-of-factly, as if it was a common thing, as if of course he could read her mind. *Can he read everyone's mind?*

"Yes."

"She stepped back, clasping her hands together to still their trembling. This is what is meant by someone wringing their hands, she thought, her thoughts so shocked, so jumbled, she fought to distract herself with trivia.

"How is it possible? Are you immortal?"

"For all intents and purposes, yes."

"So how many times have you been married?"

"Just once."

"For how long?"

"Over a thousand years."

"So she would have lived forever too, except that she could be killed? How many others are like you?"

"Not many."

"What are you, exactly?"

"Not from here. Not from this planet. Ancient legends call us Nosferatu."

"You're a v-vampire?" She stepped away again. *He is going to turn me into a blood sucking monster! Why hasn't he ever fed from me? Has he? Has he been feeding off my blood all this time?*

"No. We don't need to kill in order to live. We do need blood, but it doesn't need to still be flowing through a live vein."

"Blood bags?"

"Usually."

"Is that why you tried to keep me away from here? Were you hoping to keep me from finding this chamber until after the wedding? How fortunate for you that we've had so many storms."

"I bring the storms, Layla."

"What? How? A-Are you planning to turn me into what you are? Can you?"

"I can. I prefer you to choose to be like me, so that we never have to lose one another to death. The ancient Egyptians didn't celebrate death. They celebrated life, the eternal life that follows death."

He was going to let her choose. She could escape. He didn't want to kill her. Escape. Yes. She turned and ran from the chamber only to stop when she ran into Vivian.

"Vivian, no, we have to go. What are you doing here? Run, run, we have to go!"

Vivian hugged her. Her face was so calm, so unsurprised by her own horror. Why wasn't Vivian surprised? "It's okay, Layla," her friend said gently.

Then she noticed that Alex stood behind Vivian. "You! Did you do something to Vivian?"

"Only what she asked me to do," Alex said calmly.

"Let me show you something, love," Phoenix said, placing a hand on either side of her head.

Surprised by the fact that he was at her back, that he captured her head, she tried to struggle but found herself unable to move. Images began to flash through her mind. She was in some sort of craft, hovering above the earth. Then she was lying on soft pillows in a barge, silken curtains blowing around her as she sailed down the Nile. Her head rested on Phoenix's lap and he was smoothing her hair from her face. She was on horseback, in a large bathing pool, on a throne, and always, always she was with Phoenix.

Always . . .

***

Time no longer had meaning once she accepted the truth . . .

Layla awoke and gazed out from the top floor of a skyscraper onto a city she somehow knew was Dubai. She also knew she was on her honeymoon. She thought of her father and how he once told her about his honeymoon in Egypt, and how he and her mother loved looking at the pyramids in the moonlight. Yes, her father. Wait, he died trying to tell her something. Had he been murdered? Her heart began racing and she could barely breath. Then, suddenly she remembered that no, he had an unfortunate heart attack. Some rare congenital abnormality he'd been born with but no one had ever caught it in his physicals.

She relaxed.

There was something else though, something she . . . oh yes, she must have had a strange dream, where she dreamed that Phoenix was a vampire.

She breathed a sigh of relief.

"Thank you, Kiaria," she said, turning her head to take the goblet from her. It took a moment to register what she saw. Kiaria, and she didn't know how she knew it was Kiaria because she didn't recognize the young Asian woman who stood beside her, unclasped her fist and lifted her hand from where she filled a goblet with the blood flowing from a cut on her wrist. Layla accepted it and from what she surmised was habit, lifted it to her lips. It tasted coppery and a little salty, but overall, it was sweet and heavenly nectar.

And it made her feel alive.

The Intruder

Rob Tucker

Living alone had its disadvantages, especially when he sensed he wasn't alone.

He had never been alone before. He had been married and had children, who were now adults with families and careers. Framed photos of them populated the tops of two bedroom dressers and hung on the hallway walls. He always took for granted they were there, until they weren't. The empty frames stared back at him vacantly as he consciously searched for the photos and the memories they recalled.

At first he tried to remain calm, thinking that the missing images still existed but that he was just having some sort of minor mental lapse, a brain fart.

As other incidents occurred, he sensed he was not alone. Some presence he could not detect was in the house with him. He couldn't see it, hear it, feel it, smell it, or taste it. Whatever it was, it hovered about and didn't bother him, except for the thefts, the missing pieces.

He knew he had not misplaced his house key. It lived in the right pocket of his cargo shorts. But this time when he reached in for it, it was not there.

He tried to remember when he had last used it and where he might have put it down. When was the last time he had gone out the front door and locked it so he would have to use the key to get back in. He never locked it when he took out the trash bags to the barrels around the corner of the house. Or, if he accidentally didn't press the lower button on the lock, he knew he always had the key to let himself back in.

He did lock the deadbolt when he would go out for a walk around the neighborhood as he had done the previous afternoon. The key had been in his pocket when he returned and had stayed there until the moment he discovered it was missing the next morning.

He retraced his movements from the time he returned from his walk until he went to bed. He and his wife usually had a glass of wine and bumped into each other while they prepared dinner in their narrow galley kitchen but she had been visiting their daughter that evening and must have decided to stay the night. Yet, he distinctly remembered she hadn't called to tell him that, which led him to worry something had happened to her. He called their daughter to check and see. There was no answer, only a message that her number was no longer in service.

An alarm went off in his head. He considered calling the police, then thought it wise to give his wife time to arrive. When she didn't, he knew something bad had happened to her. He called the police and got the same message. "The number you dialed is no longer in service."

He double checked. He had dialed the number listed in the current phone book. He tried the operator. There was no response, only silence.

He thought to himself, *What the hell is going on?*

He retraced his steps of that evening, including putting dishes in the dishwasher and washing two pots and a skillet he had used during the day.

Nowhere in that sequence had he left the key on the kitchen counter or somewhere else or dropped it into another pocket or the trash. Its disappearance was less strange to him than frustrating. He opened a chest drawer that contained extra keys and rummaged through the accumulated junk of pens and paper clips and sticky note pads and medical information pamphlets. The key copy was not there. Other keys he never used and didn't remember what they were for lay in a heap as though they were soldered together but the copy was gone.

The master key was the one he had carried in his pocket. The missing copy left him without the means to lock the front door and reenter the house. He would have to have a new master key made.

He Googled locksmiths. Nothing came up on his cell phone screen. None were listed. He thought maybe there was a glitch in the software and tried again. Still nothing.

He went to the front door and opened it. He pushed the lower unlock button and closed the door, then opened it. The deadbolt button had clicked back into place. The door should have remained unlocked. He tried again with the same result. The lock had a mind of its own.

With the lock acting like this and no way to call a locksmith, he couldn't leave the house unless he propped the door open.

He walked through the kitchen to the connecting entrance to the garage. He held the door open and pressed the electric switch button to raise the garage door. It went up all right but immediately came down without his pressing the button a second time.

He thought there was something wrong with the electric system and tried again with the same result. Then he noticed that his wife's car was missing from where it was always parked next to his. She hadn't gone out to the grocery store or anywhere else that he could remember like the bank or post office.

Now, he couldn't even get out of the house through the garage, yet his wife had been able to get the garage door open and drive her car somewhere. But he was positive she hadn't left the house. So he went in search of her, calling her name.

He expected to find her sitting on the toilet playing solitaire on her cell phone while patiently waiting. She wasn't there or anywhere else, not reading a book in the TV room or mulling over a crossword puzzle or shopping on her iPad at the kitchen table. Of course, she wouldn't be in the kitchen. He had just walked through there. He couldn't remember when or where he had last seen her.

He heard the doorbell ring. Thinking his wife might be locked out, he hurried to the front door and discovered a delivery of groceries that he didn't remember ordering. He stepped outside and looked toward the street. There was no car in sight and no wife.

He carried the bags of groceries inside and closed the door. Some of the packaged items needed to be put into the freezer. He tucked them away, then shelved the canned and boxed items in the pantry cupboard. The emptiness of the cupboard shocked him. He thought it had been nearly full the day before.

As he closed the refrigerator, he heard the clatter of the garage door opening. He had not pressed the switch to open it. He rushed to open the connecting door.

The gray BMW engine started. No one was in the driver's seat. The car backed out into the driveway and onto the street. The front wheels straightened and the car sped away without a driver. He tried to envision himself in at the wheel but he was standing at the garage door entrance. He couldn't be in two places at the same time.

When his car disappeared, he knew for certain that someone was breaking in and stealing from him. He called the police. This time, someone answered. They would not come to his house to investigate just because he claimed personal items were stolen. He was told he needed to have evidence. What more evidence did they need? His car was missing, gone as a driverless vehicle racing along the local streets and freeways to who knew where.

When he turned on his computer, his files on the desktop appeared, then one by one, they blipped off the screen. He immediately shut down and tried to reboot. Everything was gone, wiped out. He had been hacked.

He didn't like to have empty hours during the day. Sleeping was okay because his hours were filled with dreams. But he wanted to fill his daytime hours with interesting activity. He couldn't think of what might be interesting.

He stared out the window at wild birds congregating at the feeder he filled with seed each morning when he went out to pick up the newspaper where it had been tossed on the driveway. Lately, the paper had not been consistently delivered. He didn't call and complain about the lapse in service because an occasional paper did show up as though the delivery person were playing a game with him. Either that or a new delivery person was just learning the route.

He selected a book to read from a stack on the coffee table. When he opened it, all the pages were blank. He grabbed another one, and then another. They were all blank.

He thought, *am I going crazy?*

He enjoyed playing piano a couple of hours each day. But on this day, when he sat on the bench and started playing, the keys he touched disappeared, leaving a black and white gap-toothed keyboard. The aborted sonorous and tinkling tones mocked him.

At that point, he began to panic. Too many coincidences of this kind were happening. The only way he could stop them was to find and destroy the presence. First, he would have to identify and trap it. He had no idea how to go about doing this.

After a great deal of cogitation, he decided he would have to outwit the presence. This would take some mental prowess. He was not cut out to be a sleuth. His efforts were not witty and he encountered one frustration after another.

In search of wit, he went into the family room and turned on the television to see what the news of the day might be. The news anchorwoman said the sun was shining with a slight chance of rain. She kept repeating herself, so he switched to another channel hoping to find a comedy.

He thought if he repeated what the comedians were saying, he would at least appear to be witty to the presence. Maybe its existence was digital. Maybe he could bring it up on the television and exorcise it by shutting off the remote.

It didn't work.

He tried to determine that if he were the presence, how could he be fooled and lured into a trap?

When his grandsons came to visit, their exuberance and noisy enthusiasm filled the house and blotted out all negative thoughts and physical pain and bad feelings. Their play and focus to be happy and focused on the moment lifted him from his doldrums.

He especially enjoyed having them snuggled at each side of him while he read them imaginative children's stories.

However, when they left, the inexorable passage of time clamped down on him. The presence allowed him only a brief reprieve. The boys could not be replaced. They had to move on.

The presence seemed to know what he was going to do before he did it. He would never succeed unless he could overcome that hurdle. The children's stories he read to his grandsons gave him an idea.

He devised a strategy that if he imagined he didn't exist, the presence would leave and no longer exist because it would not have him to feed on like a parasite. Not existing would be a mere mental exercise of his imagination like his grandsons did in their imaginary play. But when he tried it, he realized too late that he was being drawn into a trap of his own making, that the presence had set for him. He desperately scrambled to back out of its invisible clutches.

He woke out of a spell in an hallucination. He skirted the edge of a dark abyss on an endless plain. He started walking on a winding road that circled down into the darkness.

He heard children's voices yelling at him from the top of the abyss. His two small towhead grandsons stood waving at him and shouting, "Grampa! Grampa! Don't go down. Don't go down. Come back. Come back."

Since the only thing over which he did not have any control was his thoughts, he had to decide whether to go down and bring back the memories and his life.

His own voice called to him from the darkness of the abyss,

"We are your memories. You will find us here."

Leaving his grandsons behind, he stumbled down the path.

Vengeance Is Mine

Shawn D. Brink

Shane hung the receiver back on the payphone's cradle hook. The line was dead, likely because of the blizzard.

He had no idea how creepy being alone in a college dormitory could be until today. Everyone else had left Wayne State College for spring break 1989. He'd been allowed to stay behind because he was an Education major and his student teaching commitment required that he stay and teach at the public school, which did not share spring break dates with the college.

The Resident Director simply gave Shane the keys and told him to keep the doors locked at all times. His teaching plans abruptly changed though when a late-season blizzard closed the public schools, shut down the town of Wayne Nebraska, and confined Shane to Pile Hall.

Pile Hall had been built back in the 1930s and had all the old wood, plaster, and marble that might be expected in institutional construction from that era. His room was on the third and top floor.

With one hand still on the payphone's receiver, he stared out the big window near the lobby's front entrance. Outside, the snow continued to fall in ghostly torrents and accumulate in death-shroud drifts.

Shane grew hungry. There were multiple restaurants just off campus, but with Wayne gripped by the storm, such a trip was out of the question. Even if he did make it, they would likely be closed.

Instead he headed up the stairs toward his room, thinking his roommate might have left a stash of candy bars or something. When he arrived there, he froze. The door to his room was ajar.

He was almost sure he'd closed it earlier. Shane entered and conducted surveillance. The space under his bed was vacant as was the area under his desk.

I did close that door. Didn't I? Shane turned toward his closet, the last remaining hidey-hole. Just as he was almost sure he'd left his room door closed, so too he was almost certain that he had left his closet door open. Yet here it was, closed.

Being cooped in this building's just playing with my mind, he told himself. Still, I could have sworn...

He opened the closet door. Nothing was there. Nothing was out of place.

Shane entered the large closet. He parted the clothes which hung on the left rod but found nothing unusual. He then turned to his right and screamed.

Someone WAS there!

He threw a right hook and felt pain travel from his fist up his arm. A second later, he realized he'd punched his own reflection. The wall mirror in his closet, which he'd hung himself at the beginning of the term was now shattered.

"Get a grip man," he told himself. He couldn't let this isolation get the best of him.

He squatted and began to clean up the mess. A reflection in one of the larger pieces of broken mirror caught Shane's eye – a shadow of darkness that didn't belong on the white closet ceiling.

He looked up and saw an open hatch which he'd never noticed before. The cover had been pushed aside, revealing a sliver of darkness. It would have been nice to know his room had access to an attic.

I just never noticed it before, Shane told himself. Still, a shudder ran down his back.

Being alone in the dorm during a blizzard had already put Shane on edge. If he was going to sleep at all tonight, he knew he would need to investigate. Shane dragged his desk chair into the closet and clambered onto it. He pushed the cover further off to one side and stuck his head up through the opening.

Dust phantoms swirled about in the dimness, carried by trace-element gusts originating from the blizzard outside. He rubbed his arms for warmth. Obviously uninsulated, the attic was cold as a mausoleum. For a moment, he considered getting his coat, but instead wiggled up into the attic. He would only be up there for a minute, just long enough to verify that no dangers hid in the darkness – just long enough to help him keep a grip on things.

Shane didn't smoke but his roommate did, although the man never seemed to have a lighter. As a joke, Shane had started to carry a cheap disposable model so that every time his roomie was looking for a fix, Shane could offer him a light.

He now used that yellow-plastic lighter for both light and warmth, cupping his hand around the flame to protect it from any air movement. The attic revealed its secrets only as his feeble light allowed.

He took only a few steps before looking back. Light coming from his room through the hatch shone into the attic like a beacon. This was a good thing. It wouldn't do to get lost up here.

He turned forward and immediately bumped into something solid. It was an old dorm dresser. There were others as well, enough to surround the hatch, circling it like the rocks of Stonehenge. He tried to move one of them, but it was either too heavy or had been nailed to the floor.

Shane climbed up onto the wall of dressers and looked out from his perch. From his feeble light, the outlines of more dressers emerged, a virtual dorm room dresser surplus depository.

He clamored down the far side of the dresser and inhaled. The air held an odor familiar to Shane. Years ago, a mouse had died in his parent's garage. That small body had decayed for two weeks in the summer heat before being discovered. He conjectured that some rodent had met a similar demise here in this attic and was smoldering in some hidden corner.

He ventured deeper through the maze of dressers, searching for the source of the stench. If he could just find the source and document it as something benign, then all would be well and he'd sleep sound tonight.

He rounded a corner in the dresser-maze and his breath caught. Before him was the source of the odor.

The light around him began to flicker as the lighter trembled within his grip. This was no dead mouse.

The remains were in an advanced state of decay, being mostly skeleton except for the occasional lingering of residual human skin. He presumed it was female by the dust-covered, pale blue dress the mortal remains wore.

He felt watched.

Her empty eye-sockets stared, but he wondered if it wasn't something more – something glaring out at him from the attic's darker recesses.

He looked at her legs where they protruded from the bottom of her dress, shriveled and skeletal. Her feet were nothing more than a scattering of metatarsals and phalanges. Among these bones was an iron shackle that looped around the end of her tibia and fibula. The hoop was far too big to restrain the leg now but must have been a perfect fit back when those legs had been fleshed out. A chain connected the shackle to a thick support post and was secured with three brass padlocks.

She held something in her lap. Shane couldn't tell what it was in the dim light. He moved the flame nearer, but finger bones, dust, spider webs, and residual skin obscured the object.

He reached out and touched it as repulsion consumed him, but his curiosity proved stronger. He pulled the object from her grasp and it broke free with the crisp sound of mummified flesh being torn.

He brought both hands to his face, one holding the lighter and the other holding the object. It was a cassette player: the micro model that students often use at college for recording class lectures.

Wiping away an obstructive layer of dust from the little window on the lid, Shane discovered it held a cassette. Though his curiosity had reached a crescendo, common sense told him to take the recorder back to his room for further examination.

Just then, pain stung his thumb. The lighter fell from his hand and went out.

He'd been so entranced by his discovery that Shane hadn't noticed the top of that lighter growing hotter. Cooling his scalded thumb against the cold cassette player, he crouched to retrieve his only source of light. He needed it!

He felt about frantically, very aware that he was in a dark attic with a dead body. Plus he sensed that hidden watcher was still watching. Without the light, what would stop this one from growing nearer – from taking him?

In a panic, Shane abandoned his search for the lighter and stood. He could see the beacon of light which indicated the hatch's location. In his eyes, it seemed so far away.

A noise came from behind – the sound of quiet movement. Unhinged, Shane bolted, scaled the wall of dressers, and fell face first on the far side.

Pain racked him, bringing vertigo. Without waiting for the dizziness to subside, he staggered to his feet.

Jumping through the hatch, he fell onto his closet floor, missing his chair by mere inches. Luckily the shards from his broken mirror were all lying flat.

He stood up. His hands were empty. Where was the cassette player? He'd had it in the attic, but did he have it when he'd fallen?

Shane took a deep breath. He needed a moment to calm himself. He went over the facts to separate them from fiction. Yes, there appeared to be a dead body in the attic, but no, he hadn't actually seen anyone else up there. It was quite plausible that the unseen watcher was just a figment of his imagination – that the quiet sound he'd heard was only the attic settling against the wind of the outside blizzard. Even the dead body could have been a Halloween prop – Right?

Exiting the closet, his foot kicked something. There it was, the cassette player. It must have flown from his hand and skidded out into the room upon impact.

He pressed the play button but nothing happened. It was either broken, or the batteries were dead. Shane opened the battery compartment and two AAAs slid out. He retrieved his electric razor which held the same battery combination. The transfer was made, and the play button was pressed once more.

At first, there was only static-ridden silence. But then a woman's voice crackled through the speaker.

"I've not had anything to drink for days and I'm too weak to call for help. Nobody would hear me anyway. Everyone's gone for spring break. Well, not everyone. Stacey's still here, if only in my memories.

"Stacey was a Christian, so I think I'll be seeing her again shortly. It'll be nice seeing her again.

"I'm leaving this recording as evidence of what's happened in hopes that justice will eventually come. My name is Joan Parsons. I'm a student at Wayne State College – a resident of Pile Hall.

"It all started a couple days ago when the campus was closing down for spring break, 1988. Stacey and I were the last two students in Pile Hall. I was going to drive her to Sioux City. I was going there anyway because that's where I'm from. She was going to catch a bus from there to Fargo, where her older brother lives.

"I had forgotten my cassette player in the dorm room and had run back up at the last minute to get it. Stacey said she'd wait for me in the lobby. I ran upstairs, retrieved the player and put it in the pocket of my dress. Looking back now, I'm thankful I'd put it in that pocket where it went unnoticed by my abductor.

"Returning to the lobby, I discovered that Stacey was no longer alone. She was standing over by the front desk, near the corner where student mail is delivered. I stayed at the lobby's entrance to remain unnoticed. Stacey was talking with Professor Gamnon, a teacher at the college and also Stacey's ex.

Stacey had taken one class with Gamnon, and quickly became enamored. And why not? He's a young, hansom academic. Despite College policies, they became involved.

It didn't last long though. Stacey never told me why she decided to end it, not that I didn't ask but it was a subject she didn't care to discuss. To my knowledge, she'd ended it almost two weeks ago.

From my vantage point at the entrance to the lobby, I caught the gist of the conversation. She asked him what he was doing here. He answered that he'd been given the responsibility of locking up all the dorms for spring break. This didn't make sense. He wasn't a Resident Director or a member of college maintenance, but teaching faculty.

He told her he wanted to start over with the relationship, saying those cliché things that guys say, things like he would die without her love, and he would do anything to make her happy. But she wanted no part of it and I heard her tell him so.

Then, his mood changed. 'I'm not used to rejection', he said as he pulled out a knife… a big knife. He stabbed her repeatedly while chanting, "I don't like being rejected!"

It all happened so fast. Involuntarily, I let out a scream.

Instantly, Gamnon looked up from her to me. I fled, hearing his footfalls upon the marble floor as he gave chase. I tripped on the stairs and before I could get up, he was on me, grabbing me from behind and spinning me around.

By the hair, he led me up the remaining stairs to the top floor and then through a hatch in the ceiling of a closet."

Shane pressed the stop button. His hands shook with fear. He knew the Professor. He'd taken Gamnon's class just last semester. The man had always seemed so normal, borderline mundane – never sociopathic.

He recalled the news reports regarding two girls who'd gone missing last year over spring break. They had been roommates.

Glancing at the alarm clock on his desk, he realized how close to night the day had grown. Wayne State College had a murderer on the payroll, and that information was shoving Shane toward that precipice of panic, nudging him right up to the brink.

Biting his lip hard enough to draw blood, he pushed that play button and continued the story.

"Gamnon came up through the hatch. He had a chain with him which he shackled to my ankle, securing me to this post. I had to listen to him rant about the bloody carpet in Pile's lobby and how lucky it was that he knew where they kept the large remnant left over from the carpet's installation."

Again, Shane stopped the tape and stuffed the player into his back jeans pocket. Then he bolted from his room into the hallway. He slammed his door shut behind him and stood there panting – trembling.

He stared out the hallway window, desperately searching for calm in that storm, but none could be found. His hands were clammy, his thoughts jumbled.

He heard something, a thud. It came from inside his room. In terror, Shane sprinted down the hallway, down the stairs, and into the lobby. I'm alone in Pile Hall. I'm alone in Pile Hall. I'm alone... He kept thinking that statement over and over. He wanted it to be true. He needed it to be true. It had to be true. Didn't it?

He sprinted into the empty lobby and stared at the spot over near the front desk, in the corner where the student mail is delivered – where the murder allegedly occurred. He found a loose corner of carpet and began pulling. One by one, the tacks popped free. He flipped the loose corner over. The carpet pad underneath was stained a dirty red.

Wide-eyed, he stumbled back and fell over the rumpled carpet. He landed hard on his posterior – hard enough to depress the play button on that cassette player in his pocket. Joan's voice continued where it had left off.

"So here I am, left to die. All I can do now is trust in God's truth. Gamnon will die someday, and on that day he will have to stand trial for his crimes. As the Bible says, 'Vengeance is mine; I will repay, saith the Lord.'"

With that, the tape ended.

"The name's Shannon, right?"

Shane spun around. The verdict was in. He was not alone in Pile Hall.

"No, wait. Give me a second. It's Shane. Your name's Shane."

Professor Gamnon smiled as he took a step forward. He was perhaps fifteen feet away.

"I never forget a student," he said while spinning a ring of keys around on his finger and eyeing the upturned carpet. "It was a shame that Stacey had to die, but I'm sure you would've done the same, given the situation. You see, I just couldn't accept the role of jilted boyfriend."

"What'd you do with Stacey's body?" Shane managed to ask.

The professor stared at Shane, his steely blue eyes lacking evidence of remorse. "She's at rest – an intimate place just for me and her."

"She's in the attic," Shane conjectured.

Gamnon shook his head. "No, there's only one up there. Stacey received her punishment quickly. As for her roommate, I wanted death to come slower. I wanted her to think about all she'd done. She was Stacey's roommate after all and I have no doubt she played a pivotal role in turning the love of my life against me. I figured the attic was the ideal place for such reflection. Wouldn't you agree, Shane?"

Shane didn't answer.

"I'll admit," the professor continued, "I was surprised to find you here. The dorm was supposed to be empty."

Shane's heart pounded as Gamnon spoke.

"I must ask you something, Shane. Why are you here?"

Shane didn't answer.

"You see, you've made my job more difficult. I was planning on disposing of our little attic resident today. With everyone being gone, it would have been the perfect opportunity to reunite her with her roommate. Stacey's lonely, don't you know?"

Shane said nothing.

"The one in the attic is the only evidence of my secret activities other than this stained floor. And the stain is not a concern if I get rid of the body. For without the body, and with the carpet tacked back down, I doubt anyone would even discover it. And even if it was discovered, would anyone guess the stain to be Stacey's blood? Unlikely."

Listening to Gamnon's demented logic made Shane's head swim.

The professor pulled a butterfly knife from his pocket and flipped the blade out with a fluid flick of the wrist. "Actually," he said. "Now that I think about it, there are three pieces of evidence to my little crime of passion. There's the body in the attic. There's the stain under the carpet. And then there's you, with the cassette tape that I didn't even know existed until today."

Shane contemplated escape options. Running outside would be foolishness. Even if he got one of the exit doors unlocked before getting his throat slit, the professor would surely catch up to him as he tried to plow through the multi-foot snow drifts.

His only chance was to run around Gamnon and up the stairs. Once back in his room, he could try to barricade himself inside. That wouldn't be a permanent solution, but maybe it would at least buy him some time.

The murderer took a step forward. In that moment, Shane charged, feinting to the left before cutting a sharp right.

He got around the professor and picked up speed down the straight hallway. He flew into the stairs and bounded up them by twos and threes. Seconds later, he was inside his room with the door shut and locked. Running to his desk, he began to push it toward the entrance.

He didn't get far before Gamnon used his own set of keys to disengage the lock. Shane watched in terror as the door's knob turned and the killer entered.

Gamnon said nothing as he stood there, panting in that open doorway with only the desk and the knife between them. Except for the rush of their shared breathing, the room was a sanctum of silence.

Finally, the professor spoke. "Why do you guys always run?" he paused to catch his breath. "Things would be so much easier if you'd simply submit to the inevitable."

The professor took a step further into the room, pushing the closet door shut as he moved around the desk. That door creaked shut and latched into place with a soft click.

A second later, Shane heard a thud on the far side of that closet door. He couldn't imagine what had fallen in there and he really didn't care. More pressing matters consumed him at that moment.

Gamnon took another step forward, grinning. Again, there was a sound from the closet. This time less thud and more rattling.

The murderer drew nearer. "I believe this is yours." He pulled a yellow lighter from his pocket and set it on the desk.

Cold sweat coated Shane's body. Seeing that lighter brought realization. Gamnon had been in the attic when he'd dropped the lighter. Gamnon was the unseen watcher.

In his amped up state, Shane discovered he could focus on more than just the knife blade. He now noticed everything simultaneously and equally. The knife, the murderer that held it, the yellow lighter, and even the dead fly on the nearby windowsill.

There was something else as well, a quiet noise. His eyes caught movement. The closet's doorknob was turning, and the sound he heard was the mechanism within as the knob rotated. With a click, the catch released and the door opened.

Shane screamed while the professor laughed. Having his back to the closet, Gamnon had no way of knowing what emerged.

The last words on the cassette echoed over and over in Shane's mind. Vengeance is mine; I will repay, saith the Lord!

It moved out from the closet like a mist, approaching silently, staying just far enough off the floor so as to avoid scraping the lowest hanging phalanges.

Vengeance is mine; I will repay, saith the Lord. Vengeance is mine!

The professor lunged at Shane, but the blade was deflected by a skeletal hand, and missed its target. The knife was wrenched from Gamnon's hand and clattered to the floor. That's the moment the Professor realized the danger he was in. That's when he started to scream.

Vengeance is mine; I will repay, saith the Lord. Vengeance is mine!

The one from the closet was terrible. It was Joan Parsons, or at least it was her earthly remains. There was something else as well –

something undefinable that animated her corpse and appeared like a dark mist around, about and within her.

Vengeance is mine saith the Lord! Vengeance is mine!

The dark mist solidified and Shane identified it. The Grim Reaper!

A shroud enveloped the Angel of Death, its folds flapping about as the would-be-murderer-turned-victim thrashed, trying to break free from Death's grip. With its free hand, Death reached to the ground and retrieved the fallen knife. The moment it gripped that weapon, it morphed into a harvester's sickle.

As the knife transformed, so did the creature. Whereas before the dead girl had been prevalent, now the other became dominant. In fact, it was now difficult to find evidence of Joan at all. Now and then, a piece of blue dress peeked out from black folds of cloak, or a length of chain connected to three brass padlocks would flash out from the blackness – but these appearances came and went quickly.

The professor screamed the air from his lungs. His veins bulged from his neck and temples, protruding bluish against his pale skin.

Vengeance is mine, saith the Lord. Vengeance is mine!

With one fluid movement, the reaper's sickle sliced cleanly through the professor's body. Gamnon's screams ceased.

The body and the soul stood side by side, split by the sickle's blade, and frozen in identical expressions of terror. Then both evaporated into nothingness.

Next, the reaper turned toward Shane. Slowly, it put a bony finger up to its black lips.

"Shh – hush – shh." The reaper's hollow voice hissed.

Shane obeyed. He still wanted to scream, but the command of the other possessed a strange authority over him.

The Angel of Death held out his coal-black hand, flecked with white where Joan's phalanges surfaced. Shane knew what it wanted and quickly handed over the cassette player.

The player vanished from view as the reaper's long fingers wrapped around it. When those fingers reopened, the hand was empty.

"Shh – hush – shh," the reaper said again as it reached out and covered Shane's eyes with its palm.

Death lingered on that hand. Shane could smell it as those fingers passed over his face, pressing against his eyelids, forcing them to close. He wanted to push the hand away but was unable.

"Shh! Hush! Shh!" it said again, this time with more passion. Shane could smell the reaper's breath, resurrecting memories of dead mice in hot garages. "Shh! Hush! Shh!"

The darkness tightened around him.

"Shh! Hush! Shh!"

Shane could no longer hear the reaper's voice, or even sense the beating of his own heart.

Vengeance is mine, saith the Lord. Vengeance is mine. With those words repeating over and over in his head, the darkness lifted. He opened his eyes and found himself staring at the ceiling, lying face-up upon his bed, shivering uncontrollably.

He sat up and looked around. Joan, Gamnon, the reaper... they were not to be found. There was darkness outside his window. Night had fallen. The snowflakes still fell, but they descended with less intensity now than before. The storm was ending.

He turned on the reading lamp beside his bed. His closet door stood ajar, allowing him a view of the exposed opening in the ceiling. He got up quickly and closed that door.

Tomorrow, he thought. Tomorrow I will have to go up there, even though he knew he probably wouldn't. There would be no need. Everything connected to the murders had vanished, and that included the body of Joan Parsons.

He would have to re-tack the lobby carpet in order to hide that stain. He wondered, now that justice had been done, did that stain still exist?

Leaving the light on, he returned to his bed. He was exhausted. Closing his eyes, he quickly drifted off.

Just as deep sleep loomed near, he swore he heard a breathy voice whisper in his ear.

Shh – hush – shh.

Hope You Guess My Name

Ric Wasley

Father, why have you forsaken me?"

I tilted my head back and shaded my eyes against the late Judaean sun to get a better look at the man writhing in agony on the cross.

"Let me know if you get an answer," I quipped.

The men from my cohort chuckled and then went back to their dice game.

Who could blame them? Watching condemned criminals die on the cross was always boring duty for everyone. Except for me. I never tired of it.

And I had to admit that this one had been particularly satisfying as it combined two of my favorite elements to the equation - doubt and betrayal.

Doubt because the would-be prophet suffering on the cross had, after years of the utter certainty of his preaching, finally given way to doubt and despair.

Score one for our side.

And two, because I had gotten the job done by betrayal from within his own close circle of disciples.

It hadn't been easy but jobs worth doing rarely are.

It had taken me months of sniffing around under the guise of being a follower to even penetrate that closed circle of boring do-gooders and then only as a hanger-on forced to endure tedious hours of listening to him drone on about the 'brotherhood of man' and 'loving your enemies'.

Well, there wasn't one (brotherhood) and I was one (enemy) so see where that got him?

I grinned up at him and winked. "Where's you 'brotherhood' now prophet? Still love your enemies?"

He didn't answer.

It wasn't until I stumbled on the one weak link (every group has one) that I was finally able to implement my plan.

And even then, that sanctimonious fool, Judas, wasn't biting at my original offer of 10 silver sesterces - even after I doubled it. In fact I doubted he would have done it for the 30 coins I ultimately raised it to until I fell back on one of my tried and true methods, by convincing him that his betrayal actually had a noble purpose, because it served the "greater good".

I love that term. It's a favorite because it's worked equally well on the good guys and the bad. You probably know it as "the end justifies the means"... right.

But just remember, whenever you use that, it's mine. So a little "thanks" might be in order. Just sayin'.

Anyway I did finally use that to bring the dim-witted disciple around to believing that if he betrayed his master to the Romans the population of Jerusalem would rise up and throw out Pilate and his entire crew.

And in fairness to Judas, that did happen - but not for another thirty years. And by that time Judas had hung himself (he didn't even spend the silver! Idiot.) And The prophet of Nazareth had been dead and buried for three decades. Or maybe not. But that's for me to know and for you to find out. Maybe.

Anyway, it had all worked out pretty damn (forgive the play on words, I can't help it) well, and now I was just in the final mopping up stage.

And to be honest, I was beginning to sympathize with those legionaries playing dice on the prophets old cloak. It was getting boring.

I circled back to the row of crosses and checked the prophet's cross-mates. One was dead and already cooling. The other saw me coming and gave a tittle moan, then rolled his eyes, shuddered once, and died.

I have that effect on people.

That left only the Nazarene and he was the only reason I was here. So if he'd just speed it up my men could get back to the barracks and I could get on to my next assignment.

I squinted up trying to make out his features against the setting sun. He looked pretty far gone. I poked him with the butt of my spear and he raised his head still muttering about his 'father'. I sighed; this was going to be a long night.

Unless…

OK, now here is where I'm going to have to set you straight on a few things.

Contrary to what the prattling preachers of almost every religion say, I am not a sadist.

I don't really enjoy blood and guts (well maybe from far away).

And most of the suffering I induce at least has a purpose. Here it is - my classic 'means to the end'. It's not until that means has served its purpose and I get those who initiate the suffering to my end, that the real suffering begins.

Thus what I did next, despite what you've been told in Sunday school, was not out of cruelty. Quite the opposite - it was done out of what you folks would call compassion. And ok, perhaps a bit of selfish desire on my part to move things along.

I reached up with my spear and inserted the wide blade just under his right ribcage. He convulsed for a moment, then stared at me - and no, he did not utter any famous last words, at least none that I heard… though he did mutter something that i couldn't quite catch…

And then he died.

Finally.

I breathed a sigh of relief.

Time to move on.

And that's where I made my mistake.

I should have stuck around for a few more days.

But com'on. How was I to know the melon heads I left on guard duty would get drunk a couple of days later and wake up to find that someone - probably his disciples (minus Judas of course) had rolled the stone door away and absconded with the body?

Well, give me my due. It was a nice trick and I couldn't have pulled it off any better because thousands, then millions, and eventually billions believed it and it caused no end of trouble for me.

OK, now it sounds like I'm whining and that's not me. I don't want your pity just a bit of sympathy for someone who is just trying to do the job he was given. And considering the hours i put in and my millennia of faithful service, a bit of courtesy and respect wouldn't hurt either.

In hindsight I realize now that I should have done more to stamp out the prophets followers and his teachings.

After all, had't I learned my lesson more than a thousand years earlier when I let old Moses wander around in the desert preaching the same sort of nonsense for forty years?

But I mean, how was I to know - really?

But to be brutally honest I dropped the ball on that one and I did it again in Jerusalem.

Do you know they actually turned that tomb into a church? True story.

There is no accounting for taste, and I should know, I've got gobs of it.

That's probably the thing I like most about your world. Your kings and queens and especially despots, really know how to live.

And I'm always happy to watch them revel in the fruits of their ill-gotten gains, because when I get them in my kingdom, they're going to find their lifestyle more than a bit diminished.

But hey, if you can't do the time don't do the crime. Yeah - that's mine t

***

December 3, 1916

Saint Petersburg, Russia

"Grigori Yefimovich Rasputin," I sighed. "You really must be more forceful, moy dorogoy drug. For surely you are "my Dear friend" just as I am yours - Da?"

The bearded, brooding lump of a peasant stared back at me with his glaring mad eyes. For a long moment he neither answered nor moved, simply staring with those inky unblinking orbs of coal black basalt. By Satan's scaly red arse I certainly did know how to pick 'em.

Suddenly his left hand shot out from beneath is filthy robe, grabbed the vodka bottle and upended down his throat. His Adams apple moved in great gulping spasms as he drained half the bottle.

Finally he slammed it back down on the wooden table between us and giving a mighty, stinking belch slowly nodded, "Da."

Oh yes, he was certainly a gem, our mad monk.

I had picked up on him shortly after he'd arrived from the Siberian village of Pokrovskoye in the Tyumensky Uyezd of Tobolsk Governorate, in 1904. The son of peasants, crude, uncouth and a stranger to personal hygiene I'd none-the-less seen some promise in the boy and he'd caught my interest. From the lurid tales of seduction of a wide assortment of women all the way from blushing maidens to experienced courtesans he seemed to have an innate talent for selling sin.

Although he smelled like a goat he also had the randiness of one and the sting power of a bull. And in

Tsarist Russia whether you were Princess or peasant that counted for a lot.

Thus he soon found himself the interest of a wide variety of women, from countess to counter girl. And that was something I could work with.

And I did.

Under my tutelage, he had risen in status and influence to a point where his devotees now included the royal family itself. Well, at least the queen.

To be perfectly honest I hadn't seen another royal as clueless since I suggest to that adorable little ninny Marie Antoinette that she tell the starving peasants to, "eat cake."

Can you believe that? And while she did wind up in a garden party with Madame Guillotine you really can't blame me. After all nobody told her she had to add that ridiculous statement about the cake.

Oh, wait. Yeah, I guess a kinda' did. Well, then let that be a lesson on taking advice from dubious sources. Unsolicited advice is worth exactly what you pay for it and never more so than from someone who may have ulterior motives - as I always do.

Thus it was indeed all cake and ice cream to me when through some strategic bribes and few favors within the back-stabbing court of Tsar Nicholas, I was able to make the bearded satyr seem like a mysterious monk with mystical healing powers direct from the divinity.

It wasn't hard. The royal fool of a mother was so desperate so save her hemophilic son, Alexi, that by simply teaching the smelly Siberian peasant a few homeopathic hypnotic suggestions I was able to suspend if not cure the Tsarevich's disease. At least enough to make it appear that the drunken oaf from the steppes really did possess miraculous healing powers.

But being a drunken oaf and dumb as a burlap sack of beets he had pushed far beyond what I needed from him to weaken and destabilize the last truly autocratic Empire in Europe.

And yes, I do understand that Russia was not really part of European culture - just like it was not really Tartar, or Asian or Mongol or Balkan or Baltic or Moselum or Cossack, or...

And there you have it. As Churchill said, "a mystery wrapped in an enigma".

But that was neither here nor there to me. My goal was simple. Bring down the monarchy to pave the way for my best and most diabolical plan to date... Communism.

Certainly one of my better efforts if I do say so myself. And without any of the false modesty that I discourage in my dictators it became my gift that keeps on giving.

I mean who else could take a bunch of pathetic nothings whose only talent is pettiness, spite and a taste for unfettered vindictiveness for anyone not as miserable as they are, and put them in charge of millions?

Well, you get three guesses and the first two don't count. Yes... and yes again. You got it. It was me boys and girls - and a fine piece of work it was too.

More on that later.

But for now the mad, bad monk had the royal brood and their dimwitted mama right where I wanted them.

"Father Igorsky?"

That was the name I was using as a senior prelate and confessor to Rasputin. But in truth I was more than his mentor - I was his puppet master.

I mean not to brag, but the boy couldn't even function without me.

Who had to come and rouse him every morning? No, make that every afternoon? Me.

Who had to peel the rancid whores off his sweaty body and pay them? Me.

And who had to sluice a bucket of cold water over his head to wash last night's dinner out of his filthy beard?

Me again.

So was it so wrong for me to expect some kind of recompense?

I'll answer that for you.

No.

Thus when he stumbled into my room not more than 3/5th's drunk (he'd only been up an hour) and thrust the latest edition of the Moscow Times under my nose I was more than a little peeved

"What is it my son?" I said from between gritted teeth. "Are you in need of some redemption after last night's debauchery?"

"No, no ,no!" He screamed. "It's this!" He stabbed a filthy forefinger down on a pen and ink illustration which took up the better part of the front page.

It showed pointed-fanged, slobbering, leering Rasputin pawing a doe-eyed but somehow salacious Empress Katherine locked in a lewd embrace as the Empress's ample bottom pressed against piles of cash and documents labeled 'Secret German Documents' , indicating that not only was the Czarina a spendthrift but a traitor to her German roots to boot.

I perused it for a moment. It was a good caricature likeness of both of them. That illustrator I had planted in the Moscow Times had done well. Things were proceeding apace.

I savored a momentary smile of satisfaction and then composed my features and turned back to the indignant monk.

He stood there breathing heavily - his rancid breath making my chamber reek of garlic, cheap sausage and even cheaper vodka. I placed my hands over his twitching fingers.

"I understand my son, how this must wound you, but as you are innocent of all these innuendoes do not trouble yourself. God knows all and he will not judge you harshly when you come into his kingdom."

Rasputin dropped his eyes and shuffled uncomfortably from foot to foot.

"Well, there is something else, Father." He spoke slowly and uncharacteristically quietly.

"Yes, my son?"

Well, you see, father, I may have gotten a bit ah, 'closer' to the Empress than the church and the Tsar would strictly be comfortable with."

Better and better. Just as I'd planned.

But I feigned shock - it was what he was expecting. "Father Gregory!" I said it like I was horrified. Yeah - right. "Have you compromised the Empress, and your position as her spiritual advisor?"

He slammed his dirty fist down on the table. "No!"

Then more slowly admitted. "At least I don't think so."

I said nothing. I had learned eons ago that when someone is digging their own grave the best thing you can do is to hand them a shovel. So I said. "Then what, pray tell, father, is the problem?"

He looked at me and nervously chewed at the ragged ends of his mustache.

"I have just received an invitation from Prince Felix Yusupov, Vladimir Purishkevich and Grand Duke Dmitri Pavlovich to dine with them tonight at their house and I wish to know - nay, need to know, if I should attend and especially if you think they could mean me any harm."

Well, here was a happy coincidence since I had been looking for exactly such a group of useless dilettantes to neatly dispose of a crude tool who had now outlived his usefulness. So of course I smiled, warmly embraced him and said, "No - Of course not Grigori Yefimovich Rasputin. Let not your heart be troubled. I am sure that they only wish to seek your wise council on affairs of state pertaining to the continued health of the Tsesarevich Alexei Nikolaevich Romanov and your most particular friend and benefactor, Tsarina Alexandra Feodorovna Romanov."

He still had that shifty Russian peasant look in his eyes - wanting to believe in good fortune but always suspecting a trap. In Russia it was, more often than not, a wise outlook to cultivate.

However it was not the one that served my purposes at this time. I kept my right arm companionably about him as I walked him to the door.

"Go, Grigori Yefimovich Rasputin. Be of good cheer. Enjoy the mother's milk of vodkas and fine wines that these nobles will undoubtedly ply you with to share your wisdom and insight..." No one can say that I don't know how to ladle it on thick when it serves my purpose. And the mad monk lapped it up.

"In fact," I continued, "I wouldn't be surprised if these noble peers didn't have a lithesome young wench or two to winsomely serve said comestibles."

That did it. Rasputin's face flushed and he licked his lips. My Russian Sturgeon was well and truly gaffed. He would go - come hell or high water - and as it turned out, he would get both.

The next day the papers were filled with the gruesome details. According to one rather lurid account. "what really happened at the Yusupov home on 17 December will never be known".

The most commonly accepted version is that according to Yusupov, Rasputin arrived at his home shortly after midnight. He was ushered into the basement where he was offered tea and cakes which had been laced with cyanide. Rasputin initially refused the cakes but then began to eat them and, to Yusupov's surprise, appeared unaffected by the poison. Rasputin then asked for some Madeira wine (which had also been poisoned) and drank three glasses, but still showed no sign of distress.

At around 2:30 am, Yusupov excused himself to go upstairs, where his fellow conspirators were waiting. He took a revolver from Dmitry Pavlovich, then returned to the basement and told Rasputin that he'd "better look at the crucifix and say a prayer", referring to a crucifix in the room, then shot him once in the chest.

After some time they went back to the basement to ensure that Rasputin was dead. But suddenly, Rasputin leapt up and attacked Yusupov, who freed himself with some effort and fled upstairs. Rasputin followed and made it into the palace's courtyard before being shot by Purishkevich and collapsing into a snowbank. The conspirators then wrapped his body in cloth, drove it to the Petrovsky Bridge, and dropped it into the Malaya Nevka River.

Does that sound farfetched? Certainly.

But is it true? Absolutely.

You see when Rasputin had called upon me on 12 July 1914 after a 33-year-old peasant woman named Chionya Guseva attempted to assassinate him by stabbing him in the stomach outside his home in Pokrovskoye, he was seriously wounded, and doubted he would survive.

After shrieking out his prayers and getting no response to his welding and empty promises he called to me.

And I came to listen - I always do.

He begged me to save him and swore he would be my faithful servant until death. And then he added one of those clever codicils that humans always think they will outsmart me with. Don't they realize that while they've been around a few dozen years I've had eternity to perfect mine?

But they continue to try and so did Rasputin.

With a sly glint in his ferret eyes he slyly wheedled that he also wanted to be immune from any natural death, act of aggression or contagion that one man could inflict upon another.

Ah. And there you have it. The 'Devil', as it were, are in the details.

Because while I solemnly assured him that it would be so, he, like so many others did not carefully read the fine print. If he had... though to be fair between it is very small typeface and ponderous legalese that only the most dedicated law clerk could hope to decipher... he would have seen that Devils and details demand caution. A virtue of which Gregori was sadly deficient.

Thus when he had pressed a bloody thumb to the document he perhaps should have remembered that old peasant saying that, "when you sup with the devil you need a long spoon." And unfortunately in everything Gergori was a glutton. Thus he took at face value and happily signed the document that stated, "This contract shall serve to indemnify the party of the first part, one Gregori , from any all normal and natural forms of death to that which might normally befall a pious and godly man in the pursuit of his righteous duties."

He read it over once - and with some difficulty as literacy was not in high demand for a regrade monk from the steppes of Siberia. But I could tell from the narrowing of his piggy little eyes that he truly believed he'd put one over on me. Me... Humans are so arrogant. And predictable.

Because the parts he didn't pay enough attention to were the clauses about "normal and natural forms of death to that which might normally befall a pious and godly man in the pursuit of his righteous duties."

If he had he would have realized that under no stretch of even the wildest imagination could he be considered anything even remotely approaching a pious and godly man in the pursuit of his righteous duties."

Add to that the manner of his death which was not even close to being "natural and normal" and there you have it. As clear a case of nullification as ever would have had old Daniel Webster crying uncle.

But to give the mad bastard his due, when I fished his cold and sodden corpse out of the river and sent his soul to hell he didn't whine or prevaricate as so many try. He simply nodded glumly and asked what were my plans for him.

And that's how Gergori became spiritual advisor to his most Satanic majesty - right alongside Torquemada. They are quite the ecclesiastical duo.

Then it was time for Niki and Alexandra...the Romanov's.

***

Ipatiev House, Ural Mountains, *Yekaterinburg* 16–17 July 1918

"I tell you I don't like it - I just don't like it. It doesn't feel right. It's not right."

That was Boris again. A good man in fight but not the sharpest sickle in the Bolshevik shed.

But I knew how to handle him - just a raised eyebrow about his commitment to the Revolution.

"Surely Boris you have no love for these Romanov's - these oppressors of the people?"

His eyes went wide as a pair of balalaika's.

"Never in life comrade! I was there when we stormed the Winter Palace."

I smiled and winked at the commandant, Yakov Yurovsky, who had been watching the entire exchange with his usual dour expression which resembled a wolfhound having a particularly painful bowel movement.

Comrade Yurovsky, was the one who had delivered the news that the Tsar, Nicholas, his Tsarina, Empress Alexandra and their five children: Olga, Tatiana, Maria, Anastasia, and Alexei) were to be executed tonight.

Being a good Bolshevik that had not bothered him in the slightest. However the prospect of losing his soft gig as being the head jailer of the royal family and being transferred to a Red Guard unit battling the Whites across some bleak tundra had only made his grim countenance grimmer still.

No - it wasn't the execution that bothered him - it was the how.

So naturally he sought out the one person who he knew he could count on for creative solutions where questions of mayhem were concerned.

Me.

Having uncounted ages of firsthand experience with this sort of unpleasantness I was happy to do my bit.

When the royal family had been taken prisoner I had naturally been Johnny-on-the-spot and made sure that I was also assigned as one of the 14 men detailed off by Lenin to guard the royals until Vladimar Illyvitch and his cantankerous brood of squabbling Bolsheviks could figure out what to do with them.

And now after weeks of dithering, with a little surreptitious nudging from me, the word had finally come down. Liquidate them tonight - all of them.

As I said, that didn't bother commandant Yakov Yurovsky in the least.

No - the only thing that bothered this bloody minded bureaucrat, was how.

You see Comrade V.I. Lenin didn't want the royal family simply killed - he wanted them liquidated. Literally.

He didn't want a single trace left of the Romanovs. Nothing that could become a rallying point for White counter-Revolutionaries now or nostalgic nobility in the future.

He wanted all traces of them gone. Wiped from the face of the earth. Liquidated.

"What should I do?" he muttered in a soured voice as he poured himself another glass of the cheap, rank vodka.

"Kill them of course," I answered nonchalantly as I poured one for myself. I have always had a very strong stomach - a prerequisite in my line of work.

"Yes, yes," he grumbled. "That's easy enough. Shoot them, garrote them, drown them like kittens - no matter. But how do I make them completely disappear?

So I told him that too.

***

I have to admit, they all died well. Like true nobility. I guess there is something to be said for three hundred years of royal breeding. They may have been as dim as cheap bulbs and as out of touch as a hermit on a mountaintop but they all had plenty of grim spunk as they stared into the muzzles of those pistols and rifles.

I was impressed with them all - especially little Anastasia. She only screamed once as a bullet hit her shoulder and then a second creased the left side of her head matting her fine golden hair with blood.

Perhaps that was why I stood in front of her while the rest of the by now nine-tenths drunk troop of guards stabbed bayonets into the rest of the family.

Perhaps that was also why I said nothing when her limp body bounced off the truck as we turned into the small clearing where men were already digging a mass grave.

I suppose I could have said something when they pushed them all into the hole but by then they were more interested in pleasing their masters in Moscow by insuring that all the Tsar's horses and all the Tsars men could never put that family back together again.

And with the help of some axes and believe it or not, a half dozen hand grenades the task was quickly completely, the hole filled in and Bolsheviks on their way back to their vodka and oblivion.

As the weaving truck fishtailed away from the small mound of earth that was now the only kingdom left to the Romanovs I noticed that the pale body of the girl with long blond hair was gone.

I said nothing.

Later on I heard rumors that she had survived the massacre and crawled to a woodcutter's hut and eventually escaped to Germany.

So… will moralists say, "Ah-ha! Even you can be saved by a good deed."

Perhaps…

On the other hand, there is that old expression, "Out of the frying pan, into the fire."

Because Germany was the next stop on my never-ending itinerary.

***

Berlin, April 1945

I heard the rattle against the turret of my Tiger Tank. It sounded like hail or acorns half muffled by the thick steel armor, but it wasn't. It was the 7.62x.25 rounds from a Russian "Papasha" PPSh-41 submachine gun.

I looked through the sighting periscope and spotting a squad of Russians firing from the former lobby of the once elegant Hotel Adlon Kempinsk, tapped my gunner on the right shoulder and moments later an 88mm round obliterated the Russians and most of the lobby.

I do love war. Always have. All that death and destruction never go out of style. In every age and every society mankind takes to them like a duck to water or a Russian to vodka.

I know you people think that I am responsible for all of them but that's not true. Most of the time I'm not even aware until you folks have already started slaughtering each other.

True, I certainly have helped to heat rhetoric and stoke megalomaniac egos but at the end of the day it is really on you guys. You just can't stay away from it. And so far this was turning out, at least from my perspective, to be your best one yet. Truly global in scale and devastating in destruction.

Well done.

But all good things must come to end and this one was at long last winding down.

Besides as much fun as this had been I had been at it for six years and it was high time I turned my attention to some new projects.

But first I had a few outstanding contracts to close out.

***

I looked at the ruins of Berlin around me and smiled. I couldn't help it. I really had enjoyed myself in Germany over the last twenty years.

Quite frankly for sheer blind hatred and self-destructive evil the Nazis and their collaborators put even Genghis and his hoard and the Spanish Inquisition combined to shame.

Naturally with opportunities for mischief like that all around me I was quick to insert myself right inside the dark Teutonic machinery that was grinding up the souls of the soon to be damned.

I started off naturally with the disgruntled band of street thugs who called themselves the Sturmabteilung, or SA - my protégées bully boys for intimidating the good burghers of Munich.

From there it was not hard to convince a paranoid failed Austrian artist and self-styled leader that he needed an elite bodyguard. And for that I had chosen another little psychopath - a weasel in human form by the name of Heinrich. With nothing more to recommend him other than a failed chicken farm and a talent for double dealing it didn't take much nudging from me to set him on the road to hell as well.

I patted the inside pocket of my SS black leather greatcoat - those boys certainly were snappy dressers - and felt the thick stack of contracts. All were coming due and a few even past due but those were smaller fish and I'd get around to them later. Right now it was time to collect from the big fish.

"Herr Obergruppenführer," the driver called up to me. "The Fuhrer Bunker is in sight,"

"Proceed." I called down.

I had naturally chosen a generals rank and when the shooting started I'd moved over to the Waffen SS as the fighting arm of the SS, famous for their brutality and ruthlessness, afforded me the opportunity to travel all over Europe and the Soviet Union.

I never really got to spend much time in Japan but after I latched on to Hideki Tōjō, I found I could leave him in charge and the whole disciplined operation would pretty much run itself.

That reminded me, I had some mopping up to do on the other side of the world as well. But first things first.

Right now it was time to collect from one of my most promising pupils ever.

A paranoid little mama's boy that had dragged millions towards the abyss and me... Adolph Hitler.

***

The smell of bitter almonds hung heavy in the cramped room, overshadowing the perpetual rank odor of damp mold and unwashed bodies seeping beneath the cloying scent of too much cologne that usually permeated the depressing underground complex known as the Führer Bunker.

I looked over at the pathetic wreck of the delusional man who had led Germany down the road to my domain over the past 12 years and couldn't help but feel a bit of hubris.

If I could take something like this pathetic wretch from a well-deserved life of penurious obscurity and turn him into the absolute dictator of millions, well what couldn't I achieve?

There was no question about it. Outside of a closet full of neuroses and delusions of grandeur the brooding malcontent I'd picked out in a Munich beer hall in 1919 hadn't had much to recommend him.

But that had never stopped me.

Fact is, I had a long history of putting a shine on the basest of metals - and of course the opposite as well.

Adolph glanced over at the slim body of the young woman staring glassy-eyed and open mouthed at the other end of the couch.

He eyed her for a few moments and turned away muttering. "You know I think I felt more of a loss when I tested the cyanide on my dog Blondie."

That was probably true.

Outside of a passionately perverted obsession with his niece Gelli Roebells, Hitler had only contempt for women… aside from the unnatural worship of his late, thoroughly unremarkable and long dead mother - who was probably the only person to actually love him despite his emotionally stunted personality.

It was actually I who had pushed him into the relation with Eva Braun on the assumption that she would be the least distracting way to demonstrate that he was not homosexual as many rumors whispered.

I of course, knew he wasn't, because I knew that he was asexual - and outside of a somewhat pederastic lust, had no interest in sex at all.

Just like alcohol and tobacco - he had only contempt for them. His only vice was a total and complete narcissism.

So it didn't surprise me that he felt more regret over the death of his dog than he did for the vapid young woman who posed as his mistress.

I glanced over at him, brooding, head sunk on his chest, and sighed.

It was time to wrap things up.

I pulled the contract signed 26 years ago from my greatcoat and held it in front of his face.

He didn't look up but simply nodded.

I looked at my watch. The Ivans would be here within the hour and I still had many more stops to make.

"So what's it to be Dolphy, the pistol or the pill?"

He finally looked up and said in a pleading voice, "Can I do both?"

"Why not. I'm sure that Stalin's boys are on their way to bring you back to Moscow in a cage so I can understand your need to be certain."

He shuddered at that, as I knew he would, and took the cyanide capsule in one hand and his gold inlaid Walther pistol in the other.

In one last display of his signature rage that used to have Field Marshalls pissing their jodhpurs he spat, "You! You lied to me!" You promised me glory. You promised me triumph. You promised me power and adoration!"

I picked a loose thread from the lapel of my uniform jacket and flicked it away before answering him.

"And I delivered on those. Every single one."

"Ah," he glared triumph. "but you also promised me that my Third Reich would last for a thousand years."

"No I didn't. That's what you promised your deluded followers. If you read the contract that you signed," I tossed the thick sheaf of papers into his lap, "you will see that what I promised was that you would build a Reich that would be remembered for a thousand years."

"But it won't!" he screamed in frustration. "It will die with me. So you lied."

I chuckled. "Well, if you think back to your catechism from your time as an altar boy in Lindzt you will recall that the priest always warned you that I was the father of lies." I smiled as he looked stunned. Then I shrugged and yawned.

"But not when it come to contracts. No, when it come to those I am quite scrupulous. They are always fulfilled to the letter." I leaned down and stared into his mad blue eyes. "To the letter Dolphy."

I plucked the contract from his lap and riffled through the pages. "There." I pointed, "read it."

He slowly read. "and I further promise to Adolph Hitler that he will found a Reich that will be remembered for a thousand years."

I smiled. "Not 'last', Adolph…"Remembered." And it will be. Unfortunately not as the glorious empire that you swore would 'last' a thousand years, but as the most evil, murderous and insane blight on humanity that the world has ever seen. And you too will be remembered" - I smiled again - "as a monster."

It was at that moment that his spirit truly broke and melted into his final madness.

He picked up the pistol, slid back the hammer and held it to his head. Just before he put the capsule between his teeth he looked up at me, face awash with self-pity, "The German people didn't deserve me you know."

I smiled back down at him. "Yes… they did."

He bit down on the capsule and pulled the trigger.

***

After that it was just a mopping up operation as I called in my markers on the rest of the top party bosses.

I caught up with Himmler at a British interrogation center where his amateurish attempts at pretending to be a private in the Weremacht had failed miserably and he was about to be exposed.

It didn't take much to convince him of what his fate would be and in a twinkling he had taken his own cyanide capsule as well.

As for Goering I couldn't convince the fat idiot to do the same and he surrendered himself believing that he would actually be admired by the allies.

When he got handed his death sentence at Nuremberg he learned otherwise and in the end was only too happy to take the cyanide I offered him on the eve of his execution.

The rest of the slimy brood I left dangling in the wind, secure in the knowledge that they would all be mine in the end - and they were.

And I must confess that of all my minions down here they are certainly best at obeying orders with meticulous attention to duty.

And if you've ever wondered who keeps track of all the paperwork and regulations down here... well now you have your answer.

Himmler, for instance, now sits at an enormous desk listening to eternal briefs filed by an endless stream of Jewish lawyers. And the SS troops march off every morning to clean a never-ending row of clogged toilets - with their hands.

But I've gotta hand it to those boys. They sure do know how to follow orders.

***

Dallas, Texas - November 22, 1963

Let me say for the record that I really can't take much credit for Lee Harvey Oswald. He was bat-shit crazy and looser than a bag of marbles long before I got to him.

After I finished my mopping up from the war I figured I needed a break from tinpot dictators and megalomaniac messiahs so I did what most of the refugees were doing at the time and headed for the land of opportunity - the good ol' USA.

Of course I'd been there before. In fact you could rightly claim I was one of the first settlers long before the white man came with his worthless treaties and fast buck deals.

One of my best was that one where the chief of the Manhattans signed away the whole island for a bunch of trinkets and trash. But I gotta hand it to the old guy, he didn't grouse about it half as much as those Dutchmen who were convinced after one sweltering summer and bitter cold winter, that they had gotten the worst of the deal!

Anyway, during the 50's I drifted around the country for a while convincing automakers to gobble up mountains of steel to make monstrous cars with ever-increasing fins and women to wear hideous fashions with bouffant hairdos and oceans of ozone destroying hairspray.

Oh, and poodle skirts for teenage girls...? Yup, that was mine too.

I had just finished convincing a Hollywood producer that what the world really needed was yet another teenage Beach Party Blanket Bingo movie when I noticed that a particular member of the Chicago mob was becoming even more murderously unhinged than usual.

You see local mob boss Sam Giancana was telling anyone who'd listen to him and a few who wished they hadn't, that he'd had it up to his bushy black eyebrows with that Kennedy kid Jack's, brother, Bobby.

He was especially steamed about JFK appointing his kid brother as AG after he and Joe supposedly had made a deal for mob help with the election.

So Sammie was pissed. I ought to know, I had to suffer through his incoherent tirades and bad bourbon while he threatened to have the whole family whacked. Though in the end he had to settle for just one. But give him this - it was a big one.

And since I'm being uncharacteristically honest, strictly speaking it wasn't me who planned the hit, that was the Chicago mob but mostly crazy Sam Giancanaa's payback for old Joe Kennedy who had welched on his promise to have Bobby Kennedy lay off them if they swung the election to his kid.

No, all I did for that one was hunt up the most unlikely choice of hitman for the mob, Lee Harvey Oswald.

I really had to comb through my list of potential crazed gunmen and always being one to give new talent a chance to make history I think you'll have to concede that I do know how to pick them.

My role in that one was more as an instigator (as it so often is) than an active participant. Sort of like a pimp.

I procured the talent and they seal the deal.

On the other hand, bonkers though he was you have to admit that Lee Harvey did get the job done.

And Sammie G's own subsequent hit on Lee Harvey was really not my idea either. After all he would have wound up in the Texas hot seat for sure and given the mood of the country, I would have had him down here in no time flat.

As it turns out Sam found his own hit man wanna-be which wound up giving me a two-for-one with both Oswald and Jack Ruby.

Not bad for a day's work.

***

On surveying all of the chaos and history changing ramification of that incident it occurred to me that there is nothing like a high-level assassination to stir things up.

After all, it certainly got things rolling in 1914 when I inspired a Slovakian nobody to bump off the Archduke of the Austro/Hungarian

Empire which it could be argued, got me two world wars over 20 years for the price of one shot.

It also occurred to me that after devoting so much time to the Old World that I had been neglecting the New World. After all I hadn't really done a worthwhile assassination for a century, back when I convinced an over-egoed and under-talented actor to give President Lincoln a bad night at the theatre.

And just to keep things rolling I encouraged another crazy to take out Kennedy's little brother a few years later.

I had actually decided on making it a trifecta by rolling up the runt of the litter, Teddy, when he beat me to the punch by taking his girlfriend of the evening for an unscheduled submarine ride in his Oldsmobile.

After that, what could I add?

After all, it's sometimes best to give kudos to others.

I mean really, even I with eons of experience couldn't have (and forgive the pun) sunk his presidential hopes so thoroughly as the dimmest bulb on that family tree did.

I did keep an eye one that family for the next few decades but truthfully they didn't really need much help from me. They lackadaisically continued to enact their own personal "Peter Principle" curse all by themselves.

So I moved on.

It was the swinging 60's and sexy 70's and there were unlimited opportunities for creative and entertaining mischief. And nowhere were those opportunities more numerous and amusing than Southern California.

Los Angeles - September 1974

"No, no, no... Robbie baby, you're not listening to me. Here's what you're gonna do." I straightened my flowered tie and shot down the

French cuffs of my purple shirt as I admired my gold and onyx cufflinks. "You're gonna sign my boys to another album and they're gonna need something up front. Plus points... lots and lots of big juicy points."

The guy behind the big desk in the polyester patterned shirt and gold tie lowered his aviator sunglasses and looked at me over the rims.

"If I'm gonna sign your difficult to deal with and dubiously talented 'boy's' to another album, they are going to need another big hit and a major attitude adjustment."

I winked. "They go into the studio next week to record a song that Denny and Bungie have just written and I guarantee it's gonna be a number one with a bullet. It will anchor the whole album."

I leaned back in the black Naugahyde chair and put my feet up on the chrome and glass coffee table.

"And as for "attitude", well, what major rock band doesn't have its share of "bad boys" - hell, that's what fills up the stadiums and gets covers on the Rolling Stone."

Robbie, Robert Maximilian Steinberg Jr., sighed and shook his head.

"You got some set of balls on you Lou, you know that?"

"Hey, coming from a hard-ass SOB like you Robbie, I take that as a compliment."

He wasn't of course - a hard-ass that is. He was an SOB to be sure. But not the tough kind of SOB. No, he was an SOB who got there the easy way by being a 'Son Of the Boss'. And negotiating with him was like playing chess with a not-too-bright ten-year-old who had barely mastered checkers.

The old man had been tough enough and had helped me to keep my contract double dealing skills in trim when I first migrated to the victorious USA after the war.

Quite frankly I had needed a rest after that one and my overworked minions down below weren't exactly having an easy time of it either what with processing the millions of souls we'd collected over the 6 years that little dust-up lasted.

Of course they all complained bitterly. The Fascists whining about the paperwork and the Commies grumbling about the lack of vodka but hey, as I remind them, that's why they call it Hell.

Anyhow, I was glad to slow down for a few decades and loaf around Hollywood making deals for fame and fortune and getting invited to all the right parties where ass-kissing and backstabbing worked hand in glove with double-crossing and casting couch politics.

And none was better at it than Max Steinberg. He was one of my first contacts in Tinseltown when I hung my shingle as agent and manager to the stars - especially those who wanted to be one in the worst way. And that is exactly what I helped them do.

I think that Max sensed who I was right from our first meeting when after a 4 martini lunch he finally signed our first deal and shook my hand.

He glanced up at me from beneath those bushy black eyebrows and said. "I know - you're the one mama always said to never shake hands with." Then he shrugged and grinned. "On the other hand when we had our soup I hope you noticed that I did use a long spoon."

Oh yes, Max knew me and knew I'd make him rich - and I did. He also put into his personal contract with me that while he wanted me to keep the business flowing to his only son, he didn't want Junior to join him in his accommodations down the road.

I promised of course but you would think that a guy who knows to "use a long spoon", when supping with me would also know what unsigned promises are worth.

That's why I was playing with the kid now. Just like you would let a fish run out the line before yanking it back and setting the hook in firmly.

The old man had been a worthy adversary, Maximilian Steinberg Sr. He'd taken the American name of Robert when he fled Russia during Stalin's purges but everyone had always called him Max.

That's why everyone called his kid… Junior, "Robbie" - not Robert and certainly not, Max.

And I suddenly realized that playing with Robbie was not nearly as much fun as playing with Max. With Max it had been a fight with a big fish with light tackle. With Robbie it was just like shooting fish in a barrel - with a shot gun.

Time to wrap this up.

"Look, Robbie, baby. You drive a hard bargain," He looked surprised but pleasantly so, "and I love ya' kid so how about this, take 5% off my end, give the boys 2 or 3 points plus concert merchandising and we got a deal."

I stuck my hand out knowing that he didn't have the balls not to take it and of course I was right. When it comes to human nature I always am.

I got up from the couch, slipped on my new suede sport coat and started for the door.

"We'll have the contract on your desk tomorrow morning." I called back over my shoulder.

I wondered if he'd bother to read the fine print - but they rarely do.

"All right." he nodded in return. "I'll get the Art Department working on the posters for the new tour. Where are they opening again?"

I turned around and grinned.

"A brand new club that just opened off Sunset."

He picked up a gold pen from a black onyx desk set. "What's the name of it?"

"The Club Bombay." I smiled.

HOPE YOU GUESS MY NAME

"Our band the Troubadours are gonna play Bombay."

***

And the band went on to be a smash hit, opening at the Club Bombay and then touring to sold out crowds - for about six months - until after returning to the club from a successful tour it burned to the ground on their opening night, killing the lead singer and chief song writer.

After that the remaining members went into a downward spiral of deep depression and heavy drug use.

A year later they were all but forgotten and "Robbie baby" took a big loss on their tour and album that cost him Daddies business and most of his fortune.

Like I said, they all should have read the fine print.

***

Although the next few decades were not terribly exciting such as those that involved world-changing wars, catastrophic floods, famines or plagues… and before you start in on Covid just let me say… Oh pleeeze! I wasn't even involved in that one - you guys had that all to yourselves. In fact it doesn't even come up to the shoelaces of mine.

If you want to talk plagues how about the Black Death? Now that was one of mine to write home about. A few million dead form Covid? Bullshit. Try half the population of Europe from the Back Death or 90% of the indigenous population of the New World from Smallpox…? Now those were plagues.

And of course there were wars - but when haven't there been?

But once again I was only mildly involved in them.

83

Remember, I'm not like the big guy upstairs. I don't concern myself with every little detail of wickedness you people get into and I'm sorry if that bruises your frail little egos, but honestly most of your so-called 'sins' I just find laughable and truth be told...rather pathetic.

No, I confine myself to those who can make a difference for exacerbating mayhem above and beyond the average run-of-the-mill petty human nastiness.

Oh, don't get me wrong. That doesn't mean that I don't take note of those mean, selfish, back-stabbing, and hypocritical little things that the average person tries to hide from their neighbor and usually from themselves. They all get tallied up in the end - trust me. And you should see the looks on most of their faces when I present them with the final bill. Priceless.

No, it's just that I can't be bothered to get involved personally except for those cases of evil that go above and beyond the day to day casual cruelty. You know, like a Genghis Khan, a Hitler, a Stalin, a Mao or Bin Ladin.

For the rest I leave it to my uncounted millions of minions toasting their tootsies in my nether regions. They're the ones who are always there to encourage the average poor slob to cheat on his wife, stiff the waitress, bully the weak or backstab a friend.

And when they can't be wherever there is the opportunity to cause headaches, confusion and misery for the working stiff they have their own band of minions who can be counted on to screw things and make a bad situation worse. We call them lackeys. You call them politicians and bureaucrats.

So no, Unlike all the paintings and cartoons I don't really spend my days sitting around on a blood drenched throne of skulls twirling my tail like some video game version of "Game of Thrones".

No, when it comes right down to it I work pretty damned (forgive the pun) hard. And unlike the, "and-on-the-7th-Day-He-rested." crowd, I never get a day off.

Nope. 24/7 and 365 I'm on the job. I even work leap year! Keeping my pointy little nose right down to the old grindstone and doing my best to do my worst.

So please remember the next time you say, "the Devil with it", or "Go to Hell", just who you have to thank for making that all possible.

Me!

And while I'm not complaining mind you, I'm just asking for a little recognition. Because think of it this way, if it weren't for me would people be nearly so anxious to get into the other place? Just saying…

So if you meet me - and who knows, you just may - have some sympathy and some taste, because I have a difficult job and you have to admit… I do it very well.

And a little courtesy wouldn't hurt either because I have a very long list - and you never know - your name just might be on it…

Friends Don't Let Friends Die Alone

Darren Simon

Devon slowly inched his way into the side room just off from the church hall. His best friend from the time they were introduced while still in strollers lay there silently in his brown mahogany wood casket, the lid propped open. A golden chandelier above generated the only light, surrounding the casket in a protective glow that pushed back against the gloom of the dark, windowless chamber.

Devon's heart raced. A cold sweat crossed his brow. He tugged against the collar of his stiff shirt and played with his blue tie, winding it around his fingers. He didn't want to see Marcus like this, but he had to. Maybe this would help erase the horrible visions of that night.

Besides, he owed it to him to be here. After all, it was all his fault.

"I'm here, Marcus." Devon swallowed a bit of phlegm and quietly cleared his throat. "It's your best bud, Devon. I had to see you one more time."

Peering over his shoulder, he made sure no one else was nearby. He probably wasn't supposed to be here. If any of the black-robbed nuns or funeral home dark suits caught him, they'd kick him out for sure. Services were still hours away. It would be crazy then, and Devon needed time to say his own goodbyes to the one person who knew him better than anyone else. That's why he was here even if the little hairs on the back of his neck were standing at attention. Even if he could barely breathe.

The church was quiet—too quiet. And very cold. Devon just wanted to run out into the warmth of the mid-day sun, but it was wrong to leave Marcus alone.

With heavy steps, he crossed to the open coffin in the center of the chamber. Silver vases filled with white flowers surrounded Marcus. On one side of the casket was a pedestal with a closed Bible; on the other was a statue of a bloodied Jesus on the Cross, his black eyes locked on Devon.

Why was Jesus staring at him? Because it should have been him lying there, not Marcus?

The light above flickered just for a moment. Crazy timing. He froze until the light returned to normal. His body trembled. Lips quivered. His mouth was so dry, he struggled to force out a shallow breath.

Still, Jesus's eyes followed him.

He turned his head away and focused on his friend, only the body lying there in a black suit and tie wasn't really his friend—just an empty shell.

"Hey… dude." Devon stumbled over his words. He raked shaky, thin fingers through his own shaggy brown hair. His hazel eyes stung with dried tears. "I'm… so sorry, Marcus. I… can't… believe this. I didn't mean for this to happen."

His friend lay in a permanent sleep, his pale cheeks so shallow, his sealed eyes caved in and surrounded by shadowy circles. His blond hair clung tightly to his head. His expression was grave, blue lips rigid. No, this was not Marcus who had been so full of life, so full of energy—always with a briming smile, always ready for the next adventure.

"This… sucks, man." Devon wrinkled his nose. The sickening sweet odor of whatever chemical they put in dead people was overpowering. Kind of like cherry cough medicine. So that's what death smelled like? "I miss you."

He gingerly touched the smooth, almost marble-like casket. It was icy, and he quickly recoiled.

He studied his friend's sunken face. It was more like a plastic mask than flesh. Blood rushed from Devon's head, leaving him numb, almost dizzy. A pain in his gut, an emptiness that wouldn't go away, caused him to hunch over, but he kept his eyes on his friend. The funeral people—whoever had the creepy job of making somebody look a little less dead—had at least done a good job of cleaning up the scratches and covering up the torn skin.

"You shouldn't be dead, man." Devon's hands balled into fists until his brown skin turned white and his nails dug painfully into his palms. "I mean sixteen is just too young. I wish it was me instead of you, Marcus. I was in the car, too. Why did I make it? It's not fair. It's just not."

Devon lowered his head to his chest.

The lights in the chamber flickered again. A chilled puff of stale air spread through the chamber, wrapping around Devon. He couldn't help but shiver.

"Come with me. I'm so lonely."

Devon's breath froze solid in his throat. The lights flickered for a third time, casting twisted shadows across the darkened room. He tried to swallow but couldn't. The words had been faint, but the voice was unmistakable. Marcus's. Devon's pulse quickened. He slowly raised his head.

Marcus still lay there in the silent embrace of death.

"Get a grip on yourself." Devon rubbed his eyes. Was he starting to lose it now that Marcus was gone?

He stepped back from the coffin, rubbing his fingers over his clammy palms. "You're not alone, Marcus. I'm right here. And I promise to always talk to you, and hopefully wherever you are, dude, you'll hear me."

The chandelier lights flickered for a fourth time, then doused completely, casting the chamber in a shadowy layer as black as a raven's wings. Devon blinked his eyes rapidly. He should have run, but his legs wouldn't budge. From behind, the chamber's double doors slammed shut.

"Who's there?" Devon suppressed a scream—barely. He swung toward the doors, but the darkness was an impenetrable wall. He couldn't even see his hands in front of his face. "What's going on?"

"I'm afraid. Come be with me, Devon. You promised. Remember, Devon. You swore to always be by my side."

The chandelier sparked back to life but only shed a dim light.

"Come with me, Devon. Don't leave me alone on the other side."

Devon covered his ears. This wasn't happening. This couldn't be real. He turned back to the casket.

Marcus, sitting up in his casket, glared at him with glowing yellow eyes. A twisted grin crossed his lips. He extended a hand toward Devon. *"Come play with me."*

Devon shook his head. He stumbled backward. His chin and lips trembled. His legs buckled, nearly dropping him to the floor. "No! You're dead. This can't—"

"You should have died with me." Marcus slowly climbed from his casket, squirming his legs free, then slinking to the floor.

Devon retreated to the doors. He unleashed a primal scream, gripping the handles, trying to force them open, but he couldn't. Wedging his back against the doors, he turned back to his friend. "Please, Marcus, don't hurt me. I didn't mean for this to happen."

Marcus stood like a raggedy doll propped up by strings, his head dangling against his chest, arms hanging loosely at his side. Tilting his head slightly to the side, wide grin still plastered to his face, he gazed at Devon with bulging yellow eyes. Almost… inhuman. *"You have to come with me. It was your idea. It's your fault I'm dead."*

Tears streamed down Devon's cheeks. "That's not true."

Marcus lumbered toward him. His head, still resting against his chest, tilted from side to side. His smile slipped away. His mouth hung open. *"I'm so lonely, Devon. I need you with me. Take my hand."* Marcus extended a trembling hand. *"It's the only way to make it right. The only—*

"No!" Devon buried his face in his hands.

From behind the doors flung open and voices cut through the darkness.

"We have to move the deceased into the church hall, and make sure the flowers are placed correctly. Services are just a couple of hours off."

"Right, there's going to be a big gathering for this young man."

Devon lifted his hands away from his face. Two of the dark suited men from the funeral home rushed into the room.

Ignoring him, they crossed to the coffin where Marcus lay as if he hadn't just risen from the dead. Devon, his chest heaving, gasping for a breath, placed a hand over his mouth. *Oh my God, I'm really losing it*. He peered one more time at Marcus. His life-long friend rested in peace inside his coffin. He'd not just stood up from his coffin or begged Devon to join him.

Devon's mind was playing tricks on him because of the guilt. Wiping away the tears, he ran out of the chamber and away from his friend. *"Sorry, Marcus. I'm really sorry."*

***

The service at St. Mary's Church was long and ridiculous. Some fat, triple-chined priest in a white cloak stood over Marcus's casket, droning on and on about what a pious young man Marcus was.

Sure, Marcus was a good dude, a stand-up guy who was always there for Devon and their group of friends, but pious he wasn't. If there was a little marijuana on campus, he usually had something to do with it. If a prank had been played on Principal Duggin, it was a good bet Marcus was behind it. Just good-natured stuff. Nothing to hurt anyone. If Marcus wanted something and didn't have the cash, he would occasionally steal it. A Coca Cola here. A Budweiser beer there. Oh yeah, he liked to drink, too.

So, Devon had no patience for the priest's words.

He also couldn't stand all the girls from North High School's choir crying over Marcus. Before his death, not a single one of them would give him the time of day. He wasn't ugly or anything, but he was kind of thin and gawky and hadn't really come into his looks yet. Most girls ignored him like he wasn't there. They ignored Devon, too. What right did those little two-faced bitches have crying for Marcus?

Devon had watched the services from the rear of the church. He wasn't sure why. Maybe it was because he didn't want to see Marcus's mom balling, or his normally strong dad sit there with a vacant, checked-out kind of stare. Or maybe, he feared he'd lose it some more and see Marcus rise from the coffin again.

Either way, he kept his distance then.

And now, at Evergreen Cemetery, he kept his distance again from the crowd but hovered close enough to hear the priest.

"I know this young man's death is a tragedy," the plump-faced, gray haired priest said, dabbing sweat from his thick forehead. "And while we cannot understand why he was taken from us so early, just know that he has joined our Heavenly Father, and he is in a goodly place—and he is safe and in good company side by side with the Father, the Son and Holy Ghost."

"Yeah right." Devon leaned against an oak tree with his arms crossed over his chest. The thick canopy of leaves above shaded him from the worst of the late afternoon sun. Just a few pinpricks of sunlight reached the lush grass at his feet.

Still, his suit, damp with sweat, was like a heavy weight bearing down on his shoulders. He loosened his tie and unbuttoned the collar.

One thing was for sure, Evergreen really was a nice place to spend eternity. Devon gazed at the surroundings. Tall trees filled the cemetery and underneath their branches, well-manicured, almost perfectly green grass, covered the grounds. An earthy natural odor surrounded him—much more preferable to the musty stench of the church hall. There were walking trails and benches. It all would have been comforting if not for the endless gravestones as a reminder that below ground were the dead.

And Marcus would soon be lowered into the ground among them.

Sure, right now his final resting place was marked by a rainbow of flowers but just off to the side was a mound of dirt—hidden under a tarp—that would soon seal him six-feet deep. His life reduced to a headstone that would mark his birth date and death date and that he was a loved, son, brother and grandson.

If only they hadn't been so stupid. If only—

A sudden wind shook the tree, rustling the leaves and brushing against Devon's freckled cheeks.

Invisible fingers touched the back of his neck.

"Devon, don't leave me here to rot alone."

Marcus's voice, faint and almost twangy, as if spoken through a megaphone, surrounded him.

Devon spun around.

Nothing.

He was alone.

"You did this to me. Why won't you join me on the other side?

Devon's muscles tensed. A pain filled his chest. He twisted around again, and this time spotted his dead friend. Marcus stood behind his own coffin, next to the priest. Devon rubbed his eyes. It's not real. He's not there. He peered through his fingers. Marcus, dressed in his death suit with that strange grin plastered to his face, tilted his head side to side. His normally blue eyes still glowed yellow.

Couldn't anyone else see him?

Of course, they couldn't. I'm freaking crazy. Devon clenched and unclenched his fists. He scanned for his parents among the mourners. He should run to their side. But they weren't there. Why weren't they?

Without uttering another word, Marcus limped away from his own funeral deeper into the cemetery. He motioned for Devon to follow him.

Devon shook his head. His chest tightened. He banged his fists against the side of his head. *Run away. Just get out of here.* But, he didn't. On shaky legs, sweat dripping from the sides of his face, he followed Marcus, passing unnoticed by the mourners and the fat priest, and the casket that supposedly held the shell of his dead friend.

Marcus lumbered forward like a zombie, arms straight at his side, head hanging loosely as if his neck were broken. He stiffly made his way between gravestones, passing deeper and deeper into the cemetery.

Devon followed but walked a stones-throw behind. He glanced in every direction but soon there was no one else in sight. Why was he following a ghost or a mirage that wasn't really there? What did he hope to accomplish? Maybe to beg for forgiveness? Maybe, if any of this was real, he could help Marcus find some peace. *Or you could die, fool.* Wasn't that the way it was supposed to be? Shouldn't they have died together?

Marcus stopped and peered back at Devon. His yellow eyes widened. His smile seemed to split his face in half. He pointed ahead and once again motioned for Devon to follow.

"Come with me. It's the only way to make it right."

Devon stopped. This couldn't be real. His mind was fucking with him. But what if it was real? "Marcus, no."

Up ahead—what Marcus had pointed to—was a mausoleum rising above a row of tombstones. Devon shook his head. *No way. I'd have to be a goddamned idiot to go inside there.*

Intertwining his fingers underneath his chin, as if in prayer, Devon's gaze darted from Marcus to the mausoleum. From the outside, the two-story massive house of death was like the Greek Parthenon with marble white columns in the front and a towering entryway atop slick marble steps, leading to intricately carved oval doors.

Adrenaline pulsed through Devon's body, warning him to flee, but he didn't. He just stood, his eyes locking on a pair of rectangular stained-glass windows on either side of the doors, depicting Jesus rising toward the heavens.

Marcus climbed the steps, then stopped at the doorway. He turned back once more to Devon, motioning him again to follow. He still had those damn yellow eyes and that grim smile. Opening the doors, Marcus slipped inside, the doors closing behind him. Bile rose in Devon's throat. He hunched over, clawing at his neck, forcing the nausea away. His stomach roiled, but he still managed to lift himself until he stood straight.

Overhead, a patch of gray clouds swept in, blocking the sun, casting the cemetery in a blanket of grayness. Devon flinched at the sudden layer of shadows marking his path to the mausoleum.

He kicked the ground and forced himself to take a deep breath. "Fuck, Marcus. Okay, you want me to follow you inside, I'll do it." He licked his drying lips and chewed on the inside of his cheek until he tasted his own warm, sour blood.

Devon crossed the rest of the way to the entryway, sliding between cross-shaped tombstones, willing himself to climb the steps and reach for the doors. His heart pounding, lungs burning from shallow-rapid breaths, he slowly opened the doors. They were heavy and hard to grasp with his sweaty palms, but he managed to crack them open. The doors creaked and moaned in protest.

Devon peered inside.

Marcus wasn't there. No one was. Just a long rectangular hall with more Greek columns on either side stretched before him. Walls on either side held countless crypts rising from the marble stoned floor to the ceiling two stories high. Names of the deceased were carved into each. A row of round chandeliers dropped from the ceiling, shedding pale white light throughout the hall. Devon sniffed the air. His nostrils flared. The same sweet odor of chemical body preserver from the church tickled his nose.

Despite the sensation to hurl rising from his gut, he passed through the doors. "Marcus, I'm here."

Silence greeted him.

"Marcus."

"Come see what I have for you, Devon."

His limbs tingled, warning him to run, but he still didn't listen. "I don't see you."

"I'm here, old friend." The voice came from another arched entryway at the far end of the hall. "Come and see. I am so pleased to share it with you."

Devon stepped gingerly down the hallway. No matter how cautiously he walked, his hard-leather shoes thudded loudly against the stone floor. He clutched his arms to his chest to stop his body from trembling, but it wasn't working.

"Marcus, why are you doing this to me?" He inched closer to the entryway. With each step, an icy chill wound tighter and tighter around him, squeezing his insides until he couldn't breathe.

"We belong together."

"Why?"

"It's only fair since you killed me."

Devon shook his head. "I didn't. It wasn't my fault." He reached the entryway and crossed into another hallway lined with crypts.

Marcus was there.

He stood just beyond the entrance to the side hallway behind an open crypt. His arms were outstretched to Devon. His yellow eyes glowed brighter. His smile remained. But his face was different. Devon's eyes fluttered. His heart crashed inside his chest. The flesh was torn from Marcus's cheeks. Shredded skin hung loosely, draped against his neck. Devon's head swooned. Dizziness overtook him. A gash spread across Marcus's forehead. Dried blood matted down his hair. Drops of green mucus and puss slid from his nose and mouth.

"No, this can't be real." Devon's legs buckled. He dropped to his knees.

"Look, Devon, I have found a place for you to rest… forever… just like me." Marcus tilted his head to one side. His eyes never blinked. *"All you have to do is take my hand, then climb inside, and we can be together on the other side, the way it was meant to be."*

Devon lowered his head to his chest. He tugged on his hair, then looked back up. "No, Marcus, please. I don't want to die."

"Oh, but you must." The smile faded from Marcus's face. *It's only fair. You killed me. You killed me. You killed—"*

"Shut up!" Devon sealed his eyes and pounded the marble floor with his fists over and over. *"Shut up… shut up… shut up."*

When he opened his eyes back up, Marcus was gone. The crypt was closed. He was alone again. There were no signs Marcus had ever been there. Devon laughed wildly. He curled up on the floor, rocking himself until…

He spotted a drop of blood where Marcus had been standing.

His laughing stopped, replaced by hyperventilating. Gasping for air, he scrambled to his feet and ran from the mausoleum.

***

Devon lay on his bed in his darkened room, sheets pulled up to his neck. He searched his thoughts for any recollection of how he got home from the cemetery. What the hell had happened since he ran from the mausoleum? He couldn't remember eating dinner, seeing his parents, or even walking upstairs to his room and lying in his bed.

He gripped his sheets until his knuckles turned white. What was happening to him? Sure, the wreck messed him up. Shit, it took his best friend from him, and his life would probably never really be the same. But why was he losing his mind? The guilt? The sadness?

Or was it the visions of that night he couldn't shake when they slammed into a car, and Marcus's head smashed through the windshield. The sound of metal crunching in on itself and the clamor of shattering glass rang in his ears. Marcus's blood and brain matter dripping from the shards of glass haunted him.

His friend's death was the last thing he saw before blacking out. *I never should have woken up, but I did. And now Marcus is coming after me. No, he's not. Stop it. You're just fucked up, man, and you've got to shake it.*

Devon rolled onto his side. His eyes wide open, he stared through his bedroom window at the fog that rolled in sometime after dark. The mist blanketed his neighborhood in an unnatural crimson glow as it mixed with the hazy streetlights. He checked the clock on the dresser beside his bed—1 a.m., according to the blue digitalized numbers. *I've just got to get some sleep. So damn tired.* But if he closed his eyes, the visions would return.

"Screw it." He forced his eyes closed. "I have to -"

The doorknob on his bedroom door clicked once, then twice... and a third time. Devon's heart skidded to a halt. He shut his mouth, sealing in his breath. His body tensed. The door squeaked open. No! Please! Not again! The sweet stench from the church and the mausoleum filled his room. A tear slid down Devon's cheek. Oh, God, why!

Trembling, he slowly opened his eyes. The door was closed. He was alone in the darkness of his room. He placed his hand over his aching chest, willing his heart to beat again. He opened his mouth and sucked in a lungful of air, then slowly released it. He shook his head and let a nervous chuckle slide from his lips. Maybe, it would be a better idea if he slept with the light on.

He turned over toward his dresser to switch on his lamp.

Marcus, his torn face bleeding onto the blankets, lay there beside him, his twisted grin wide, his yellow eyes glowing brighter. "Don't leave me alone." His voice was little more than a whisper.

Devon screamed and rolled out of his bed, falling onto his backside. He retreated on his hands and knees to his door, gasping for a breath. *"Marcus, leave me alone."*

Marcus slithered from the bed, his body undulating like a snake. His head dangled loosely from his neck. *"I'm so lonely. Join me, Devon. It's only right.* Marcus extended an arm toward Devon. *"All you need to do is take my hand."*

"No!" Devon reached for the door, threw it open and stumbled into the hallway. "Mom, Dad, help me!" He ran to his parents' room, ripped the double doors open, and thew himself at their bed. "Mom, Dad, wake up. I need help!"

No one answered because no one was there.

Their bed hadn't been slept in. The covers were untouched.

Devon gazed through the darkness in every direction. *"Mom… Dad, where are you guys? Please, I need you."*

"Take my hand, Devon."

The words came from the doorway. Devon swung around. His dead friend stood there, his body more shadow than substance, his glowing eyes illuminating his pale, shredded face. Black goo dripped from his lips. Devon's mind spun. The only thought that made sense was to escape. But how? Marcus blocked the door. He struggled to breathe. His chest felt like a fifty-pound weight pressed against it. *Mom, Dad, where are you? Oh, God, I need you!* He clenched his jaw. His arms and legs shook violently.

Marcus limped toward him. *"Devon—"*

"Leave me alone!" Devon peered over his shoulder at the large window across the room. That was his only way out. All he had to do was unlatch the window, punch out the screen, climb onto the second story roof, and jump to the grass below. Then run… and never stop.

Heart pounding like a sledgehammer in his chest, a cold sweat across his brown, he swung toward the window.

"Devon, wait. Please don't leave me. I'm not going to hurt you. I'm just so alone and need my best friend."

Devon lowered his head. His hands balled into fists. He turned back to Marcus. His friend's arms were outstretched to him. The weird smile on his face was gone. The shredded skin and black goo dripping from his mouth had also vanished. He looked like… Marcus, except for the yellow eyes.

"Please come with me. I promise it's not so bad, and we can be best friends forever." Marcus took a step toward him. *"Devon, I forgive you for killing me. I really do. Please be my friend again."*

Devon dropped to his knees. He placed his hands over his ears. He couldn't hold back tears. "Marcus, I'm scared. I don't want to die."

Marcus's smile returned. "But you have to."

"No!"

"Yes." Marcus limped forward until he was an arm's length away. *"Just take my hand and all will be as it should be. You'll see."*

Devon gritted his teeth. He struck his forehead with his palm. Maybe Marcus was right. Maybe this was the way it was supposed to be. Why go on living with the guilt? Why face the horrible visions? "All right, Marcus." Devon extended a shaky hand to his dead friend. "I'll come with you."

"All will be right now." Marcus's grin widened. His yellow eyes bulged. He reached out and gripped Devon's hand.

Then tugged Devon close until their faces were inches apart.

"Come with me, my friend." Marcus hissed out the words. This close, his breath was putrid. More black goo dripped from his lips. Devon tried to free his hand, but Marcus tightened his grip.

Then the change came.

Marcus unleashed a wild scream. His body spasmed. Bones cracked. Chest heaved. The flesh on his hand liquified, dripping over

Devon's. Trying to jerk his hand free, Devon cried out and fell backward. Marcus still held him, his hand now a charred, blackened claw with long, thin spiked nails, slicing into Devon's skin.

"Marcus, stop!" Devon sobbed. His body quaked.

"Don't be afraid, friend." Marcus's mouth dropped open until his jaw unhinged with a crunch. One by one, his teeth fell from his loosened mouth. Devon tried to look away, but unseen hands forced him to look at his friend. Invisible fingers kept his eyes from closing.

God, help me! Devon shook his head.

Blood and puss poured from Marcus's lower lips. With his free claw, he plunged razor sharp nails into his own cheek and tore away the skin as if it were nothing more than a mask.

Devon screamed. Marcus squeezed his wrist tighter and pulled him closer. *"Look upon the friend you killed."*

Underneath Marcus's torn skin was more charred flesh and exposed bone. Black circles surrounded his glowing yellow eyes. He ripped away his scalp and hair, revealing a gray, withered brain covered by magots.

"Marcus, I'm so sorry." Whatever unseen force held his head in place finally released Devon. He lowered his eyes. "Forgive me."

"All is forgiven. Now, we will have so much fun together— forever." The voice no longer belonged to Marcus. It was high pitched, almost childlike, and the words were sung more than spoken. "You're my friend forever… forever… forever…." The singing gave way to a cackling laughter.

Devon, still on his knees, slowly raised his head. They were no longer in his parents' bedroom. They were back in the cemetery. He knelt at Marcus's fresh gravesite, his view beyond limited by a thick fog that boxed him in on all sides. The only light came from the glowing eyes of the charred beast that stood over him, now without clothes, his body little more than a skeleton covered by rotting flesh. Was this

Marcus? Was this what he had become in death? Devon shook his head. It couldn't be.

Placing his hands against the cool granite of Marcus's gravestone, Devon peered up at the creature. A mix of rage and fear sped up his pulse. "What are we doing here?"

The creature smiled at Devon, revealing rows of yellow fangs and a spiked tongue. More black ooze slid from its mouth. "Look there, my forever friend." The beast pointed to an open grave next to Marcus's with a headstone already in place. *"See what is written there. It's my gift to you for killing me."*

"Stop saying that!" Devon took a shaky breath and leaned closer to the gravestone. His muscles froze as he read the words etched in a curved slab—*Here lies Devon Taylor, the best friend anyone could ever have—even in death. Born Dec. 12, 2005. Died May 25, 2021.* Devon gasped. It was today's date.

"It's for you, Devon. Now we can be together forever." The creature lowered its head to Devon and placed a bone-thin blackened arm around his shoulder. Devon's insides turned to ice. He shivered, trying to break away from the beast—or Marcus—or whatever this nightmarish thing was—but it wouldn't let go. *"Devon, we can cross over together. The way to the other side lies within."* The creature jarringly shoved Devon to the edge of the grave. *"Just let yourself go, and we will be together for eternity."*

Devon peered into the hole—and found himself gazing into a void. There was no ground below. Just an endless tunnel. Hot air with the stench of rotting eggs rose from the nothingness, striking his face. He pushed back against the beast only to have the creature bury its nails into his side.

Devon shrieked. "Let me go! I don't want to die."

"You promised," The beast whispered into his ear, pushing him closer to the hole. *"Friends forever—for all eternity. That's what we will be."*

"No! What are you doing?" Devon struggled, writhing along the ground to escape.

The beast kissed Devon's cheek. Its lips burned. "It's time."

"No, please!"

Laughing wildly, the beast shoved him into the bottomless grave. Devon's panic strengthened his limbs. Stretching his arms to their breaking point, his hands dug into the earth at the top of the grave. His body clung to the side, feet dangling into the void. *God, I don't want to die like this!*

The beast hissed just above him. Devon, his arms burning, hands shaking, peered up. The face of his friend Marcus glared down at him. "Devon, I died because of you. Friends don't let friends die alone. Now, let go and accept your fate."

"No… this… can't… be real!" Devon tried to pull himself up, but his arms were quickly weakening. He tried to steady his feet against the side of the grave, but the mud gave way, and his legs slipped. His fingers were losing their grip, sliding from the earth. His shoulders were cracking "No, God, save me."

Pained moaning rose from the emptiness. A hand wrapped around his foot. Then another… and a third.

The beast above, still with Marcus's face, cackled louder. *"Oh, what joy, Devon. More friends have come to welcome you."*

"No, please!" Devon shifted his gaze below. Glowing eyes climbed from the darkness toward him. More hands, the flesh withering away, tugged at his legs. The moaning grew louder. *I… can't… hold… on! He hyperventilated. He turned his bulging eyes to the foggy night. Good…bye, Mom… Dad.*

The beast held out its arms. "Don't be afraid. Cross over with—"

A glowing blade pierced the beast's chest. Marcus's face contorted in pain. The beast's body convulsed. Throwing its head back, it unleased a terrible ear-piercing cry, then its body slumped. Lowering its head to Devon, the beast spoke with Marcus's voice. *"I just wanted my forever friend."*

With a final long breath, the beast slid from the glowing blade and dropped into the hole, his body quickly slipping from view.

Two hands, illuminated in a golden light, gripped Devon's wrists and tugged him free from the monstrous hands below. Whoever held him easily lifted Devon, then gently lowered him onto the ground. Devon shielded his eyes from the stranger's blinding light. He peered through his fingers but could only see an outline of a being.

His legs, weak and exhausted, couldn't hold him up. He dropped onto the grass, bowing his head to his chest. His pulse raced, and he couldn't stop his body from trembling. He struggled to breathe. His lungs burned.

"What's... happening?" Devon kept his hands over his eyes.

"Aye, lad, you're safe now. Breathe easy. Those bloody demons are a real pain in the ass, but they won't be bothering you any more today."

Whoever saved him spoke with a booming English accent. Devon tried to lower his hand, but the blinding light stung. "Who are you? I can't see you."

"Oh, my pardons, lad. Is this better?"

Devon gazed through his trembling fingers. The searing light dimmed to a soft white glow, revealing a tall, nearly transparent stranger in a white robe. The stranger's face was hidden underneath a hood. A sword hung at the being's side. "Who are you?" he repeated, his voice shaky.

The stranger slowly removed the hood, revealing a man with an elongated face covered by a thin red beard. A thick mane of red hair flowed from his forehead down to his shoulders. He had blue eyes, which studied Devon like a concerned parent. Devon lowered his hand. His racing heart slowed. He sucked in a lung full of air. For the first time since what seemed forever, he felt... safe.

Confused as hell, but safe.

"Lad, I am Gabriel, and allow me to offer my apologies for not coming to your aid sooner." The glowing man bowed to Devon. "I would have come sooner, but these damned, bloody demons are running amuck. They've kept me a bit busy, they have, but that's no excuse for my late arrival."

Devon's head spun. His stomach churned, and he felt like me might be sick. Clenching his body, he forced away the sickness. "Are… you… an… angel?"

The man in the white robe smiled slightly. "We don't really call ourselves that where I come from, but if that term makes you comfortable, then we'll use it."

Devon tried to stand, but his legs wouldn't support him. "I don't understand any of this. Why did my friend Marcus do this to me? None of this makes any sense."

"Oh, lad, that was not your friend. No, sir." Gabriel placed a hand on the glowing hilt of his sword. "No, that was a demon, and he had his sights set on you, my boy. And he almost had you, too. When you submitted to him and took his hand, that's all he needed to drag you to an eternity of suffering. Lucky I arrived when I did. Those demons are nasty things. They desire to claim a human soul as their own, and they prey on the recent dead and their confusion. Those bloody bastards can even change their form, and they'll fight each other like mad dogs over their human playthings. No, that was not your friend Marcus. It was a demon deceiving you, making you see images, like your friend, that weren't real."

Turning his head to where the open grave had been, Devon froze. The hole was gone as if it had never been there. Grass replaced it— not even an outline of the bottomless pit remained. The moaning had also ceased. The only sound was Devon's breath, Gabriel's booming voice and the rustling of leaves caused by a gentle breeze that started to sweep away the fog.

Devon gazed up at the stranger. "You saved my life."

Gabriel's thick reddish eyebrows bunched together. "No, lad. I saved you from the demon. But, my boy, you're already dead."

The cool breeze gained speed, whipping Devon's hair against his forehead and cheeks. He wrapped his arms around his chest. What had Gabriel just said? I'm already dead? That wasn't right. It couldn't be. How could he be dead?

He brushed the hair from his eyes. "No, I survived the accident. Marcus is the one who died. He kept saying I needed to join him because I killed him."

Gabriel, his robe blowing in the wind, shook his head. "No, lad, your memory is a bit off. Common really. It happens to a lot of you who are new to the afterworld and are awaiting ascension. And the demon played on that. He used your foggy memory against you. Weakened your spirit, so he could drag you down to the lower world. Fact is, my boy, Marcus is the one who survived the wreck. You did not. The sooner you accept that, the sooner your spirit will be able to ascend to an afterlife beyond your imagination."

"No, I can't be dead." Devon crawled on his hands and knees to Marcus's gravestone. "Look, this is where Marcus was buried."

"Lad, look upon the writing etched in the stone." Gabriel knelt beside him. "This is your final resting place, not Marcus's."

Devon gripped the smooth stone. His eyes grew wide as he read the words. *"Safe journeys to our beloved son, Devon Traylor. You will always be loved. Born Dec. 12, 2005. Died May 5, 2021."*

He placed his palms against the side of his head. He bit his upper lip, biting through the flesh until his own warm blood ran down his chin. "No, this can't be. You're playing games with my mind. I'm not dead. Look at me, I'm still flesh and blood."

"Only in your mind, lad." Gabriel lowered his head. "Much of your confusion is because I wasn't here to guide you right after you died. That was part of my job, and I failed you. I promise never to again. But, if you need more proof, place your hand upon my shoulder. I will reveal more, but it will not be easy for you to see."

Devon, his head numb, gut aching as if he'd just been sucker punched, reached up for Gabriel's shoulder. His thoughts spun wildly. How could any of this be true? What about his family? Where were they? Why couldn't he just wake up from this nightmare? Why wouldn't it just end? His hand grasped Gabriel's shoulder.

"Hang on, lad." Gabriel uttered. "This will be a bit unsettling."

"It can't be any worse than the shit I've already experienced." Devon tightened his jaw, his arms and legs. "Let's do this."

"As I said, lad, this will not be easy for you to see." Gabriel lifted his sword overhead and waved it around and around. The blade glowed brighter with each circle, humming as if coursing with electricity.

The world around Devon began to spin with each rotation of the blade, faster and faster. A dizzying display of lights exploded before his eyes. As if caught in a vortex, his body twisted in every direction. He couldn't tell what was up or down or if he even still held onto Gabriel's shoulder. Bile rose up his throat. He was going to be sick if this wild ride didn't end soon. And then it stopped as jarringly as it began.

His head jerked backwards. His vision skidded to a halt, but the dizziness continued. His brain ached. He placed his palms against his temples to stop the pain. At first, his sight was blurry, then it started to clear. His surroundings came into focus.

Devon's mouth hung open. His eyes, now fully focused, stared without blinking. Oh my God. They stood at the intersection of a busy city street under the cover of a night sky. They had arrived at the scene of an accident. Devon's accident. But how? Hadn't this already happened? "I don't understand. How—?"

Gabriel, his hands hidden within his robe's sleeves, gazed down at him. "In the afterworld, time does not exist as it does among the living. We can move in time, but we cannot change what has already transpired. We have returned to your accident, which, to the living way of thinking about time, occurred two weeks ago. We are here but not really here. None can see us. We are… ghosts, as the living call us. Do the memories begin to return, lad?"

Devon's heart beat heavily within his chest. Each breath came slowly. Marcus's father's car was flipped over in the middle of the intersection, the driver side smashed into a mess of twisted parts and broken glass spotted with blood and what he could only guess was bits and pieces of brain matter. Another car, its front end demolished, was just off to the right. Police and fire crews surrounded both cars.

Devon lumbered a bit closer to the wrecked vehicles.

Gabriel walked beside him. "Do you remember what happened that night?"

Devon stopped. A body lay in the street covered by a blood-soaked sheet. He didn't dare walk any closer. "Is it Marcus? Have you brought me here to show me how I killed him?"

Gabriel placed an arm around his shoulder. "Quite the opposite, lad. See for yourself. AS I told you, your friend survived the accident." Gabriel pointed to an ambulance a few car lengths away. There, Marcus sat in the back of an ambulance. His forehead was bloody, but he was very much alive… and crying.

So, who was underneath the sheet?

Gabriel lowered his head to Devon. "Tell me what you can about that night. Try to think clearly."

"Who's beneath the sheet, Gabriel?" Devon inched closer to the sheet. His body trembled. Sweat dripped from his brow.

"First tell me what you remember, lad."

Devon sighed. He closed his eyes. "Th… there was an end-of-the-year award ceremony at school. I got some silly award for history or something. That's why I was in this stupid suit." His lungs sucked in more air. His head pounded. "Soon after we got home, Marcus showed up at my house. He had taken his father's car without permission, and he'd smoked a little weed. He was in no shape to drive. Hell, he didn't even have his learner's permit yet."

Gabriel nodded. "What else?"

The memories flooded his mind, crashing like waves against his skull. Pain spread across his forehead as if someone was hammering a nail through his skin into the bone. He pressed his palms against the side of his head. "I didn't want Marcus to get in trouble, so I told him I'd drive the car back to his house. Hell, I'd had a learner's permit, so I figured I could handle it. I told him somehow we'd sneak the car back onto the driveway." Devon stepped even closer to the body. "Oh, God, why did I do that? How stupid could I be?"

Gabriel scratched his beard. "You were trying to keep you friend out of trouble."

Devon didn't look up at Gabriel. He knelt to the body. "I don't exactly know what happened, but when I was driving through this intersection, another car smashed into us. I remember the sounds of the smashing glass and twisting metal. I think something hit my head." He strained to remember more, but his memories slipped into the fog of time. "What happened, Gabriel? Tell me." His eyes fixed on the bloody sheet over the body.

Gabriel sighed. "Lad, you were struck by a drunk driver. It wasn't your fault at all. You didn't kill Marcus. He is alive and healing. In fact, the exact opposite occurred. Devon, you died that night."

Devon reached for the sheet. He recoiled once, but then grasped it. Taking a deep breath, he slowly lifted the sheet away.

And found himself staring at his own body lying there crumpled on the street, his skull crushed, revealing part of his brain. Devon gasped and fell backward. His dead body was missing his right eye—the socket a shattered bloody hole. The skin along his cheeks was shredded. Bone fragments stuck through the skin. More blood seeped between his lips. Devon covered up the face, then buried his head in his hands. *Oh, please, no!*

He sobbed wildly, rocking back and forth. It was all clear now. He'd died that night, not Marcus. He had no future. Marcus still did.

When he was done crying, he swallowed a lungful of air as he sat by his own body. He wiped his eyes and fought off the sickness of seeing his own broken face. No reason to be sick now. No reason to cry any more.

At least there was comfort in knowing Marcus had survived.

Numb, unable to stand, he gazed up at Gabriel. Perhaps there was still a chance. Maybe there was reason to have hope. "Gabriel, you're an angel. Can you give me one more chance? Can you help me get back to my body? There're still so many things I haven't done. I want to live."

Gabriel placed a hand on Devon's shoulder. "I'm sorry, lad. I don't have that kind of power. What's done is done. You have to accept your fate now and move on to what lies ahead for you."

Devon nodded. "I understand, but I want to see my parents first. Gabriel, can you take me to them, so I can say goodbye?"

"Sure, my boy, let's be on our way." Gabriel threw his arm around Devon, then lifted him to his feet. "But take heart, lad, because something wonderful awaits you."

"What is that?" Devon studied Gabriel's kind face.

"Now you and I can be friends forever—for all eternity."

Devon froze. "What did you say?"

"Friends forever, Devon, the way it was meant to be." Gabriel smiled. It was a smile wide enough to split his face in half.

Death by Mummy

Francesca Quarto

"Are ye proud of yerself, ya ninny!"

James Dunner was livid, and not about to let his mate off the hook for what he saw as his total lack of good sense.

"I specially told ya NOT ta open da caffin until Matilda got 'ere ta keep tings on track. Now, 'tis awake en on da loose."

He would have said more, but Matilda McDonough poked her frizzy gray head into the shed. "I come as fast as ever I could, lads."

She was panting like a newly run greyhound, her thick body throwing off waves of heat as she bustled into the dimly lit outbuilding belonging to old man Dunner. He held a tiny croft near the village of Bailycline. Not much by way of a farmstead. His only livestock, a few motley sheep, a dozen barren chickens, one lazy rooster and a milk cow he called, Bertie, after the Queen's adored husband.

"Now, what's all dis I been hearin' from da gossips? 'Bout yous two boys findin' a caffin in yonder woods? En why have ya sent fer these old bones? "

"Yer our onlyest hope, Matilda, at findin' dat ting as got out; afore it does some wickedness 'pon the village folk," James answered with sincerity spread across his face like butter on warm bread.

"Stuff 'n nonsense ya speak, James Dunner! I aint no sort a magic user, 'n dare's da truth a it!"

James opened his mouth to respond to her denial of having extraordinary powers, but his partner, Paddy O' Laughlin, jumped into the verbal fray. His high-pitched voice causing the chicken that had followed Matilda into the shed, to flee.

"Tis not us sayn' ye use dark arts, Matilda. Nay! Tis whispered 'ear 'n dare, 'bout ye sailn' ore' cottage 'n woodland, like a wee boat on dark waters! Tis said, ye sit astride a black cat, screechin' like a horny owl!"

This lively conversation was only interrupted long enough for old Dunner to retrieve his jug from his cottage adjacent to the shed. This required shooing away the broody appearing sheep, Bertie, the cow, as she wandered back to the dusty barnyard along with the sheep from their day of munching on his neighbor's garden, the frustrated chickens, and the lazy rooster that seemed to sleep through every sunrise since he hatched.

Returning to the shed, now even warmer with the bodies sitting around on various stools and barrels, the liquid was most welcome to the animated discussion.

"I ken see ye 'ave a right badly perdikment, lads, 'en because I know a wee bit o' folk remedy, I ken lend a bit a help. Firstly, ye 'ave told me naught regardin' who ya found lien' in yonder caffin."

The long wooden box in question was leaning precariously against the back wall of the shed, which was also leaning precariously. It was obvious from the shattered lid, that it had been pried open none too gently. This occurred during Paddy's haste to retrieve any rings or baubles buried with the deceased. The story he related to Matilda left out the part where he was scavenging for valuables.

"Tis like a bad dream, Matilda," he was saying with a wispy voice.

"James 'ere, left me wit da caffin, as went ta look fer a crowbar, or da like. We planned ta pry away ta lid, ta see who twas rattlin' round in dare! Whilst 'e was off searchn', I taught I heard a scratchy kinda noise comin' from da box! It skart me plenty, I tell ya! I woulda run ta fetch James back, but I knew it might be better ta see if 'twer a livin' bein', buried, afore e's time!"

Paddy took a deep drink from the jug as it was passed to him from Matilda, who herself had quaffed a good quarter of the heavy brew.

James sat on his stool, looking over at the empty coffin while listening to the tale. He was shaking his head slowly from side to side, as if in denial of the story as it unfolded. His eyes were only slightly blearier than the storyteller's.

Paddy wiped froth from his mouth on his rough woolen shirt. "Well, I used me brute strength 'n tore open ta lid, ta let in some fresh breeze don't ye know. I looked inside ta hole, and me breath clogged in me troat like mud on a pig! Ta bloody body were wrapped like a rag doll as far as I could see! I pulled away them other pieces 'n afore long, I was lookin' at a giant, wavin' long, rag-covered arms about, en pullin' is own self out da caffin! I near pissed meself I tell ya true, en only me 'ere ta stop ta raggedy brute!"

His two listeners were nodding their heads, making sounds of alarm and fear, but that was mostly due to the level of brew left in their jug.

"Ah, Paddy," Matilda finally said, leaving a loud hiccup to finish the comment.

"We need ta find da rascal afore it can do a mischief!" James was slurring a tad, so the words sounded foreign to his friends who merely nodded knowingly.

"It appears ye do need me wee bit o' magic lads! I'll be back in da shake of a lamb's tail."

Matilda rose from her perch to her plump, unsteady legs and exited the shed. Good to her word, she was back in a thrice of a wag, cradling a round iron pot with a heavy felt for a lid.

"Tis 'ere is me own magic brew, lads. It'll bring dat livin' dead creature back 'ear ta 'is caffin. When 'e comes, we put 'im back into 'is box, en carry it back ta where James found it."

They all nodded agreement with this fine plan, and Matilda proceeded to remove the cloth cover. The contents of the black pot let off an odor so pungent the three gave a collective gasp. Matilda studied the faces of the two friends, speaking as from a pulpit said, "Praps we'd best test a wee sip afore dat ting returns."

The villagers were holding their own search the next day, because three of their folks seemingly disappeared in the night. They scoured the countryside, avoiding the deeper parts of the woods. No sense was seen covering ground none of the missing would have gone. A few searchers reported seeing flashes of white floating through the woods, and thought again about chasing after such an enigma.

When one of the search party returned to the village for two hunting dogs to aid in the task, he passed directly by James Dunner's old shed. He was taken with a vague, but unpleasant odor wafting out of its partially opened door. Approaching to investigate the source, he threw open the door and let out a scream. Many of the other villagers were nearby, not wanting to leave the village unmanned entirely. Upon hearing the cry, they came pelting back to Dunner's croft.

James, Paddy and Matilda sat on their barrels and stool, stiffer than the boards around them. Each clutched their drinking cups like an owl would a mouse. Their eyes were fogged over with the vacancy of death, for which there was no outward cause. The village constable and a doctor from two villages over, were sent for, post haste. Both agreed the trio "...looked like they'd seen sum kinda monster, or ghost." Besides the bugged-out eyes, their mouths were all twisted in silent howls and screams.

The only bit of evidence found at the scene of the mysterious deaths were pieces of white rags clinging to the rough wood around the door. The constable named it a case of poisoning by a putrid batch of spirits, but the local crofters had a different take on the deaths.

Late in the day, when the sun colors their fields in purple and crimson, many a farmer has reported seeing a human-like form shambling through the surrounding woods, wearing long white rags around its body and limbs. If anyone knew the truth of the deaths, they were certainly keeping mum!

Hyenas

Rob Tucker

The pack had been trailing him for the past three days. He managed to elude them by finding temporary shelters. He had to keep moving, but in his weakened condition he could no longer run to get away. Always, they watched him to see if he would stumble and go down. They watched for the opportunity to approach him and close in.

He needed food and water but his escape route had taken him farther from such resources. There was nothing and no one in this wilderness to help him. That alone demoralized him almost to the point of just giving up and letting the pack have at him. But the thought of such a painful end terrified him.

The will to survive still flickered weakly within him.

He regretted having left the camp in search of something better. At least there he had the security of enough numbers to ward off predators. And there was food and water. He had taken enough when he slipped away during the night. Leaving at night had not been a good idea. Predators prowled and hunted at night.

His flashlight batteries weakened. The fading light dimmed, just enough beam left now to see the pack's glowing eyes when he shined it at them. Hoping they would not be able to find and follow him, he stopped using the light.

They still had no trouble of course because of his rancid scent. He had not washed or bathed for many days. He had gotten used to his own smell but it lured the pack attracted to decay.

Others at the camp had stayed clear of him because of his illness. Their avoidance had been a factor in his decision to strike out on his own. He was familiar enough with the terrain to find places to hole up, but with the pack watching and waiting at his heels he needed a good place to hide, a place that sheltered him and provided a source of food and water. Such a place was hard to find, so he had to keep moving.

At one point he thought he had lost the pack, but still did not relax his vigilance. They might discover some other prey. They were crafty and persistent, but ever hungry. They would appear again, undaunted, unless he could find a sanctuary.

As he stumbled on, his worn soles barely protected his feet from the bruising rough stones. The blistering sun raised heat waves from the dry cracked ground. He looked around for a patch of shade among the brush and sparsely foliated trees. Finding the shadow cast by a spindly tree, he lowered himself to its base. He imagined a spring of cool water bubbled up from between the roots. When he reached out to touch it, the spring wasn't there.

He closed his eyes and slept.

The shuffling steps and guttural grunts from the pack awakened him. He smelled their foul breath and stinking bodies as they closed in. He pulled out his knife and slashed at the nearest one that dared to approach him.

The pack fell back.

Fear of the knife kept them at bay.

He knew the moment he fell asleep again they would attack. He could not let that happen.

Bracing himself against the tree, he tried to stand but his knees buckled. His head raced with fever and vertigo. He lowered himself to the ground. There was nothing more he could do. The confrontation was a waiting game.

He struggled for an hour. Then two. But despite his effort he lost consciousness.

The pack carried him further down the flood control channel to their encampment under a bridge.

They roasted and feasted on his flesh. deaths, they were certainly keeping mum!

As Good As A Blind Man's Candle

Francesca Quarto

"Ah, yes. There's a story to be told this night, but are you all certain you have the steel in you to hear it?"

The men regarded Patrick with sly looks, trying to judge the Englishman's sincerity in the matter of a promised Halloween tale. The six rough looking ranch hands lounged around a large campfire on this brisk October thirty-first. Some still scraped their tin plates clean of beans with hunks of corn bread, while others sipped coffee strong enough to wrestle a steer to the ground.

Patrick was the camp cook. He'd been riding behind the ranch boys in a covered wagon loaded with supplies for ten days This was his third cattle drive. They were moving twelve-hundred head from their ranch outside Santa Fe to the nearest railroad yard, with several days of rough terrain in between. They'd been eating his grub for the better part of two years and still didn't know much about the old coot.

He had a strange way of talking that somehow prohibited them cursing or spitting in his presence. Even though he ate their dust most of the trips, he somehow managed to stay clean and tidy looking when they rode in for their evening meal.

One such night, the youngest among the saddle-sore cowboys asked Patrick if he was "...some kinda doc, with that fancy talk ya got?"

In his usual quiet, unhurried manner, he answered that among other things, he had been a thespian on London's finest stages.

"A what?" the youngster blurted.

"An actor, young man." After the crew learned of his past profession, a few shyly began asking him to entertain them with stories of his exotic former life while they sat around the fire eating their mean meals.

This night was no exception. It was the youngster, on his third plate of beans, hoping to secure another minuscule piece of salted pork who spoke up as he settled on a log close to the fire. Patrick seemed reluctant at first, telling them, "Stories of Hallow's Eve are best told on any other night! Recounting tales of spirits and ghouls, encourages visitations from ghosts who roam freely this night."

The six men, reeking of leather and cows even in the sweet mountain air would not be dissuaded, insisting they were not fearful of "nothin' without a gun!" as the young man stated firmly.

And so, Patrick settled in, choosing the log the others always left vacant for his expected story-telling each night.

"There was a gentleman of great wealth, his mansion tucked into a corner of a small Shire, twenty-odd-miles distant from London. He was a powerful man in this county, made-up mostly of scrub-farmers and cottagers struggling to make a living at one of the businesses he owned. In his own village, that business was the unique Candle Emporium Factory. Understand, this was an innovative concept for the times. Fine beeswax candles were created by many hands, in many different sizes, shapes and even colors. These were sold throughout the region to Churches, civil servants, and any private residences that could afford them, rather than the rough-made tallow candle of the poorer classes. The wealthy man designed the special molds and refined the dipping process himself, but all that was before his accident."

"What kinda accident?" the young cowpoke sputtered, corn breadcrumbs scattering into the campfire.

"He was injured gravely when one of his candle molds literally exploded from excess use and heat, splashing liquid wax onto his face and into his eyes. His eyes were sealed shut for several minutes before the wax cooled enough to remove. By then, his eyes were scalded to the point they no longer had any color but looked as white as the underbelly of a dead fish."

The youngster drew in his breath at this description, the others smiling to themselves at his queasy nature.

"The wealthy owner was whisked out of his busy factory by his manager, a blanket over his head hiding the severe damage done to his face by the molten wax. The workers later spoke of the smell of burnt flesh hanging in the air for hours after. The injured man returned to his large house for the long convalescence his physician recommended. The doctor secretly held little hope for much healing and couldn't bring himself to completely remove the bandaging. Several weeks went by with the doctor checking daily on his patient's progress. He reported on the workings of the candle making business but gave scant information on the man's slow recovery from his burns, merely keeping watch for any sign of infection showing on the bandages.

After a month spent resting and sitting quietly in his gardens, the man grabbed for the doctor's hand as he began to re-wrap the top gauze covering his face."

"Undo the bandages, Dr. Phips! All of them this time! I have had enough of this languishing about. It is time to move on with life!" While he sounded optimistic, the man knew he'd been blinded and likely, greatly disfigured. The doctor wondered at his positive attitude toward what would surely prove a disastrous outcome.

Phips stood behind his patient in the rich surroundings of his bedroom. He slowly began to unwind the long gauze wrap."

"Well come on then...whatd' the doc find, Cookie?" It was the impatient young cowpoke again, squirming on his log to hear the answer to a man's fate.

"Why, he found the rich man's eyes were sunken! Two black holes looked back at him from a face covered in angry red scars made by the rivulets of hot wax. The doctor couldn't repress a gasp of utter shock at the hideous visage he gazed upon. He didn't know how to respond when the man asked him why he hadn't removed the covering from his eyes but stood mutely until the frustrated patient lifted his hands to his face.

"There are no bandages here, Phips! So, I am truly blind." He ran his hands over the deeply carved creases and mounds of scars on his once handsome face. "You may leave me now, Doctor Phips. I know what I needed to learn."

"What in God's green acre does that mean?" hollered the young cowboy. His question bounced off the hills around them and the others heard a few of the cattle lowing into the darkness with their answers.

"The rich businessman had prepared for this moment. He knew his chances of ever seeing again were as remote as the Orient to him. He would turn to the occult, a mystery from his past. He'd been a foundling and was told most of his life his parents were drowned in a river boat accident. But after he amassed his great fortune, he used it to hire private detectives to unearth the truth about their identities. Accessing county records and old Church documents, they discovered his father was leader of a cult that adhered to the teachings of the ancient Druids. His mother was among its first members. Together they forged a band of thirteen men and women who pledged their lives to the mystic life, using magic to serve their dark purposes.

The rich man, sitting day after day in the isolation of his eternal night, decided to reach out to the last living member of those Druid followers. Her identity was unearthed along with his parent's buried past. She came to see him after he sent word to her. Bush, his manservant, brought her to his rooms, staying on to witness their strange meeting.

The injured man told the old crone he would have his sight restored, shouting, "I know you were part of my father's coven of thirteen Witches! You have the power to do as I command. I want to see as well as my mother and be as handsome as my father."

She responded in her raspy voice, "I ken do fer ye, ma Lord. I needs only a single candle from yer precious shop."

He didn't question her, but sent, Bush, hovering nearby, to his factory to fulfill her odd request."

One of the cowboys got up from his seat to put several logs on the fire before it burned out completely. They were all so immersed in the story the cook was narrating, no one noticed how the years seemed to fall away from his animated face while he spoke. He resumed as soon as the man retook his seat. The flames jumped up as if excited at the prospect of finishing the tale.

"When Doctor Phips had packed up his medical bag, he was quick to leave the great house and its deformed owner. The wealthy man, having confirmed his worse fears, knew it was time to implement his plan. He rang for his manservant once more. This time he was ordered to go into the woods on the outskirts of the village, to locate the Druid Witch. Bush could barely look at his Master's face and the blackened orbs that once held his blue eyes. He tucked a fine woolen blanket around his legs against Autumn's chill, stirred the fire in the hearth, and left the house on this desperate errand.

Coincidentally, it was Hallow's Eve...as it is this very night! Bush heard the shrill voices of some village children, as they went about their Halloween mischief in the square and around the cottages. He soon stepped into the deep, green silence of the woods, breathing-in the sharp scent of pine and the loamy odor of decaying forest debris. There was a full moon riding high on its black stead of night. It created thin pools like curdled cream upon the dark, lumpy earth.

He'd heard village gossip of a Witch living alone in a hovel, near a small running brook. Bush stopped for a moment, listening for the sound of the burbling water, over the sound of the crunching leaves he trampled. He was about to take another step, when he felt a soft brushing near his ear and smelled a sour breath of air.

"Do yer young Master send ye fer me?"

The man-servant almost watered the ground in his terror at the old woman's sudden appearance."

The young cowpoke snickered, as the truly immature will tend to do. The Cook ignored this and continued. "He has asked that you come immediately, woman!"

The toothless crone cackled at his pretense of courage. "Ye return by yer own path, boy," she told him, leaning heavily on a long, carved tree limb and moving a few feet off. Bush could hear her begin to chant in a strange language. He was greatly relieved to be getting away from the filthy hag, turning for a second to look back at her hunched figure. In that instant, the Druid Witch shot up above the trees. He watched as her black silhouette crossed the face of the moon, sitting astride the walking stick. The sight inspired the poor man to run as if the Devil could smell his fear. He returned to the mansion, taking the marble steps two at a time. He rushed into the Master's Sitting Room where he'd left him in front of the fireplace a mere hour past.

The blanket lay on the floor. The chair was empty except for a small wax figure. Bush slowly moved closer to the strange object, glowing a pale white on the rich brocade of the chair. He reached out his hand, picking it up carefully. His face got close enough to make out its features. The scream erupting from Bush's mouth bounced off every wall of the empty house. He tried to throw the wax doll away from himself, but it clung tenaciously to his hand. He banged it against the arm of the chair, but it wouldn't become dislodged. He ran around the room and then the house, trying different methods of prying it lose, cutting it off, even trying to melt it.

Finally, exhausted from his long night of terrors and exertions, Bush found himself back in the Master's Sitting Room. He threw himself into the chair, closing his eyes for a moment to gather his wits.

When he opened them, he saw the room had gone completely dark. The glow from the fireplace was gone and not a shred of moonlight penetrated the heavy velvet drapes. Bush felt like he'd fallen into a bottomless well. He struggled to breath. He no longer felt the weight of the wax doll hanging from his hand. He had to learn the truth of his situation. Reaching his hands up, he felt the ragged ridges of scaring covering his entire face. His fingers moved upwards, finding the empty orbs where his eyes should have been. Now he understood why it was his own face he saw carved on the evil wax doll. He was meant to take his Master's place in this eternal black pit that was to be his life."

One of the cowboys had nodded off somewhere in his story, but the others were as silent as sleeping dogs at the conclusion.

Until the youngster spoke up. "That there's a crazy story, Cookie! I figered it out some, when ya said that Bush fella saw the wax doll. That's where the candle went, right?"

Cookie stared into the young cowpoke's eyes. "Why you are a clever boy! But one thing you need to know. Every Halloween the candle must be replaced to keep the rich man alive and in his current health."

"Well, we sure don't need no candles out here!" the young man responded, laughing at his own wit.

Cookie's hand slid into his pocket where it poked about until his fingers wrapped around a single, stout candle. He smiled at the innocence of youth and bid them all happy Halloween.

The Opal Ring

Elizabeth Alsobrooks

Jasmine accepted the white dove from her father's outstretched hand, smiled and gestured toward his gold-turbaned, bowed head as the gathering tourists clapped in appreciation.

The marketplace was crowded for midweek, especially during the slow season. She was glad her father insisted they do a quick performance to generate additional interest for tonight's show. Hotel bookings were climbing again, but that didn't guarantee a full house with so many other entertainment choices available in Cairo.

The talent scout was coming tonight. He had to believe her father could pack in the guests if they were going to get the Vegas contract. It was her father's lifelong dream, and she would do anything to get back to America and away from Uncle Hassam.

Jasmine slipped the dove into his cage, picked up the three rings and handed them to her father with a grand, graceful gesture, and smiled at the crowd before backing away. She had become quite a dutiful magician's assistant since they moved to her uncle's hotel after her mother's death six years ago.

Her uncle worked hard on transforming the American-born teenager into a subservient Egyptian female in his male-dominated household. He might have had better luck if she didn't have such clear and fond memories of a loving, independent American mother. Of if she didn't have a father who adored and cherished his wife, and still mourned her passing. Jasmine knew about the locket with her mother's photo that he kept in his pocket and took out to gaze upon at odd moments, when he thought himself in solitude. It had his photo too. She knew because she gifted it to her mother for her birthday the year before she died in that terrible automobile accident.

Glancing down, she moved her hand from her left wrist where she absently rubbed the thin, vertical scar, now hidden by a permanent henna-hued tattoo of a Siamese cat trailed by little kitty paw-prints, the sun above its head dissected by a pentagram.

"Sheba," she whispered, feeling the silky brush against her ankle, thankful for being pulled back to her duties by her faithful companion.

Since only she could see her, the cloaking spell Jasmine used as added protection for her beloved feline assured Sheba's access to even the most secure locations.

She reached for the rings, gestured toward her father, smiled, and walked through the crowd, holding out a small hat to receive expected courtesy tips, glad for once that she was wearing the face veil. She didn't appreciate the rest of the tourist expectation costume that made her look like a sexed up belly-dancer.

It wasn't just her uncle's ass-grabs she had to worry about now that he'd convinced her father he'd boost his sales if she wore this, and her father wore traditional magician garb. Her costume, graciously provided by her uncle, was little more than a skimpy bikini with transparent slit chiffon over her legs and arms, and a matching chiffon veil for her face and head. If only she could transport herself into a bottle to hide once in a while. She had to get away and soon, or it would be too late.

"That went well, don't you think?" her father asked.

"I was surprised at how many were here today," she said, handing her father the money.

"No, you keep it, Jasmine. I have more for you, too. You'll be needing some things for our trip to America." He laughed then, and Jasmine joined him, feeling an odd flicker of hope wriggle against the steel wall she had built around her heart six years ago. She hadn't seen her father's smile reach his eyes since her mother's death.

"A wonderful act. Certainly grand and attention-grabbing. I'm not quite sure about the finale though. Something more over the top is necessary to sustain the crowds in Las Vegas. They're fickle and have such a diverse range to choose from. I'll be able to swing back in four weeks. Let's see if you can come up with a show-stopping final act by then. How's that?"

"Fair enough," her father told the scout.

Eavesdropping from behind a set screen, Jasmine couldn't help the slight droop in her shoulders as she let out her breath. It wasn't a crushing blow, but it was a disappointment. They both hoped the man would offer her father a contract on the spot. Still, he promised to come back again, a return visit in just four weeks, and tourist season would be high then. She mustn't give up.

Sheba taught her that. Shortly after her thirteenth birthday when she was missing her mother and feeling particularly alone, Sheba, a tiny, bedraggled stray kitten adopted Jasmine. On that same day the feline continued to rub her little head against an old trunk until a small drawer popped open as though the cat had purposely revealed the secret compartment.

Jasmine discovered her mother's Book of Shadows hidden in the old costume trunk. With it, she learned to enhance her father's magic with her own, just as her mother had done. It encouraged him to focus on his magic again and turn less often to the bottle and other means of numbing his grief.

She left the stage and slipped into the service hallway so her father wouldn't have to face her until he'd had time to compose himself. Despite his polite response, she'd noted the disappointment in his voice. He hadn't touched any alcohol or opium in over a year and promised Jasmine he was done with it for good. She knew he was trying. He spent more time with her, becoming more like the father she remembered from her childhood before her mother's death. His magic continued to improve, too.

Her father was a fine magician, but with the aid of true magic, he performed feats that slight-of-hand entertainers could only mimic. She thought her power strong enough, but clearly she was wrong. To secure Vegas and escape her uncle, she must take no more chances.

She needed to go speak with Ahmed, the hotel security assistant and Jasmine's best friend since she was an orphaned little girl in a strange land and he a scared new houseboy in a large casino hotel.

"What has you so distracted, little mouse?"

Jasmine froze.

She refused to look up past the gleaming brown alligator loafers blocking her way. What was her uncle doing here? She took this hall to avoid him. Why hadn't she smelled that cloying musk he always wore? She stood in the shower for an hour to rid herself of its memory whenever he touched her.

"Kitty got your tongue?"

"What do you want?"

"Respect. We can start there. I gave you and your father a home when he lost everything to grief and a bottle. And worse. Do you remember that?"

"I remember everything." She looked up at him with defiance then, fueled by anger and undisguised hatred.

"That American arrogance. It's going to get you in over your head yet, little miss," he said, reaching out to grab her shoulders.

"Take your hands off me!"

He shook her like a bobble-head doll, until her neck felt like it might snap. Then his meaty hand slapped her face so hard her head bounced off the wall. Her neck hurt. It felt sprained. Her head throbbed. She blinked, trying to focus her vision, her attention.

"S-stop."

And then he was smashing his wet, drooling mouth against hers. She tried to pull her mouth away, tried to suck in air, to breathe, to survive. He grabbed her ass, his fingers brutal and bruising, jamming her against him, lifting her up so he could grind up and down against her crotch.

He turned, carrying her with him and slammed her back into the wall, wedging her there with his body weight, freeing his hands to mash her breasts. She jerked her head to the side, causing a spasm of pain to shoot down her back from the kink the twist put in her neck, and she gasped and gulped in air.

He raised his head and snarled through a vapor of stale cigar breath, "You need to learn your place. You will respect your elders and do exactly as you are told. Do you understand me?"

"No, leave me alone," she managed to rasp out in a broken whisper.

He squeezed, hard, crushing handfuls of tender flesh beneath his brutal domination. "I said, do you understand me?"

"I understand that you're a monster. Let me go!"

His attention focused on her nipples and he squeezed, twisting them until she cried out in agony, sure he would rip them from her body, "Please, no, stop, let me go."

He loosened his hold and then began to caress her breasts, still aching from his savagery. "That's better. You see. It can be nice or it can be not nice. It's entirely up to you. All you have to do is learn to be respectful."

"Please, just let me go," she pleaded, hating him for what felt like a lifetime of vulnerability, humiliation and helplessness. If only she were stronger, or her mother had lived long enough to teach her more.

She needed that talisman!

Her magic made her feel stronger. It gave her the confidence she needed to overcome her immobilizing fear of him. She wasn't strong enough to escape and prevent him from sending his network of thugs in pursuit of them. Not yet. If her father got a job in America, he wouldn't dare interfere, and by the time he realized the move was permanent it would be too late for him to prevent it.

To her surprise, he lowered her to her feet and said, "For now. Think about what I said." Then he turned and walked away. Trembling, she rubbed the lump on her head. Feeling dampness, she pulled her fingers down and saw that they were red with blood. "Damn you, Uncle Hassam. One day you will pay for this," she murmured. "I promise you."

Unfortunately, she knew why he let her go. He enjoyed toying with her. He enjoyed feeding her fear. The continued torture escalated her horrified anticipation of what was to come.

He'd been doing it for six long, endless, agonizing years, since she was twelve and first came to live with him in his foreign land with his unfamiliar customs and rules and foods and laws. She was terrified the first time her uncle put his hand under her dress and caressed her over her underwear, holding her in place when she tried to move away. The first time had been brief. Over so quickly she was confused. But later, he held onto her and continued his fondling despite her protests, scolding her until he was finished, on his terms. And she had let him, in the end, too frightened and confused by his foreign language and rage.

At first she complained to a loving but distracted father, who tried to listen but smelled strongly of alcohol and some pungent smoke she didn't recognize as tobacco but understood made him sleep and forget his pain. Then he woke and then spent time with her mother's photo and his magic tricks instead of a daughter who had her mother's eyes and hair and smile, and who had a nanny and tutors and maids and servants to look after her.

So she tried to tell others. Those who looked after her had been so appalled, so aghast, and so affronted by her confession. They told her she must be confused. Her uncle was providing her with a home, food, and security. She should be grateful. In the end, she felt ashamed, mistaken, ungrateful, disloyal, and wrong.

Then, as she grew a little older, he grew bolder. He drew her across his knees, and pulled down her underwear and spanked her, hard, for any imagined infraction, when she was well past the age of being spanked. He held her in place, despite her protests. His hands punished, then lingered and caressed and wandered and offended, and terrified her tender young flesh.

That's when she finally complained again. Her father and everyone else was appalled, so aghast, affronted, she must have misunderstood. There was no way it was possible anything like that actually happened. If only her mother had lived, had been able to explain such things to her. She was just confused.

Yes, Jasmine had agreed, if only.

The housemaid found her just in the nick of time they said, and it was a wonder her head hadn't sunk below the water line in the bloody bath. All Jasmine really cared about was the fact that it seemed to keep her uncle under control for a while, at least until recently.

She rubbed the henna-hued tattoo on her wrist and stumbled down the hallway, the opposite direction from the man she hated most in the world. He had made his intentions clear enough. Yes, it would be too late to escape his total domination of her body very soon. Very soon indeed.

***

"You're sure it's the one from the scroll I've been studying?" Jasmine asked.

"It must be. I've never seen anything like it," Ahmed said softly.

"But why would it just be for sale like that, like a trinket? Oh, if only it could be true, right now when I need it most, Ahmed."

"It's the right era, the right design. The crazy merchant can't know what it is, I tell you."

"It's got to be a knockoff," Jasmine insisted. "Do you know how many cultists would kill to get their hands on this artifact? It's been missing for centuries. Let's hope it's real. We have to make sure the merchant never figures out it's not a knockoff."

Feeling a sudden premonition that she was being watched, Jasmine looked around the narrow, crowded street of the marketplace. A few Bedouin in brightly colored robes led camels down the street a few shops ahead of them. A vendor to her right shook a broom at ragged street urchins who kicked an empty can too close to his display of Persian carpets. The rich aroma of freshly brewed Turkish espresso wafted on the afternoon air and combined with the scents of exotic spices, florals and tobaccos.

Ahmed turned and raised his head. "Let's grab something to eat before we head back, too. I haven't eaten yet and I smell fresh goat meat."

"How can you think of food at a time like this? You are always hungry."

"Okay, sorry. Come on. It's going to be fine. What have you got to lose?"

"My entire life savings, and the last chance I have to escape that monster, that's what," Jasmine snapped.

"I'm sorry. I didn't mean to make light of it. I was trying to ease your mood. I know how important it is. I would do anything to get you away from him. I'll do whatever it takes, you know that."

"Well, let's go see." Jasmine pulled the hood further over her face and darted into the so-called antiquities shop, known for its touristy knockoffs.

The two co-conspirators noted the proprietor, a portly Arab in colorful garb descending upon them with eager salesman demeanor. They browsed random artifacts, with feigned disinterest.

"Ah, would you like to buy a lovely necklace to grace the swan-like throat of your beautiful maiden companion, my good man? This very day I have acquired a necklace worn by Cleopatra herself, a gift from Marc Anthony. Or perhaps you would prefer a brooch, a jeweled scarab to bring you good luck."

"Just looking. Thank you," Jasmine said. "I don't wear much jewelry. Maybe a paperweight?"

"Oh! Such beautiful paperweights! Statues of Isis, Anubis, Osiris, the pyramids, come, see what we have. Right this way!" he said, gesturing toward the back of the store.

Jasmine dutifully followed, examining a few of the items he suggested, shaking her head and setting each one back down as if it wasn't what she sought.

Ahmed, an aisle away, held up the ring they had come seeking and said casually, "This is different. I don't suppose you like this?"

"What is it?" she asked, walking over to look at it.

The merchant followed, eager for a sale. "Oh, we just got that in a few days ago. An antiquity, from a long lost pyramid, the dealer assured me. A magic ring. See how it shines," he said.

Jasmine reached for it. "Oh, I don't know. It's an opal, isn't it? And I think it's a fire opal, too. Aren't they a soft stone, easily broken?"

"No, no! Very strong. A gemstone. See how they have carved a pretty star shape into it? Can they do that with a soft stone? No! Very rare! It belonged to a god! A Pharaoh!"

"Close," Ahmed muttered softly.

Jasmine kicked him behind the merchant's back. "I don't know. How much? U.S. Dollars of course."

"U.S.?" She could practically see the dollar signs blinking behind his greedy little eyeballs. "Very rare. No less than $1000.00"

In Arabic Ahmed said, "$100.00 take it or leave it. We know it's a knockoff."

"$200."

"150."

"175."

"Sold," said Ahmed.

Jasmine handed the merchant the money and they left the shop with a priceless ancient gold and pentagram carved opal ring. Legend said it once belonged to King Solomon, brought to him as a gift from God by the Archangel Michael himself. Legend also claimed that this fire opal held within its fiery depth power over the fiercest Jinni the world had ever known. The wearer of the ring could command the magical Jinni to do their bidding.

***

"I don't know what has come over me lately, Jasmine, but I feel like I can perform even the most difficult feats flawlessly, like when your mother was alive. I want to practice the tiger act today. When the scout comes tomorrow, I want to perform it. I think it will assure me that Vegas contract," her father said.

"I think you're right," she agreed, smiling. She saw Ahmed's look of concern and turned away. It was all worth it and everything was turning out better than she could have wished. Nothing in life was free. If she had to give away all her jewels what did she care? She still had a beautiful opal ring, and it was all the jewelry she would ever need. Just let her uncle try to come near her now.

She hurried around backstage, putting the equipment away. As she sprinkled some birdseed into the dove cage feeder, Ahmed said, "What happens when you don't have any jewelry left?"

Jasmine glanced up and said, "I thought you were working the night shift. Don't worry so much. I just buy more, silly."

"I swapped with Mullah, and I'm worried about you. That's what friends do. So what if you don't have enough money to buy more jewels? What then? Have you thought of that? I think we might have made a mistake." His brow creased with concern and the usual sparkle in his golden eyes darkened with worry. "Don't use the ring again, Jasmine. Please. Give it to me and let me sell it. I can get more than enough money to buy tickets to America."

"No. My father won't just leave. He has to get this job. I can't leave him here. Uncle Hassam will turn him back into an addict in no time. He has no idea how evil his brother is. Uncle Hassam is nothing but friendly and solicitous in front of father. He sees his offer to handle all our business affairs from the hiring of my tutors and nannies to father's tailor as a family kindness, not the controlling and manipulative act it is. I'll manage somehow. I will. I must!" Jasmine set down the feed and turned to Ahmed.

She looked down at the ring that seemed to dwarf her hand and felt suddenly heavy. Cupping her right hand in her left as though to support it, she looked him in the eye. "He's doing so well now. You said you would do anything. Did you mean it? Then support me in my decision, Ahmed. The scout comes tomorrow. What if he turns father down again? Would you prefer that we kill my uncle to get my father away from the evil that surrounds him? To get me away from my uncle's evil intentions?"

"When I think of--"

"Ahmed! You promised not to do anything rash." She grabbed his clenched fist and drew it to her chest until he relaxed his grip.

"No. No, of course not," he said with resignation.

"Then please just support me in this. I am under enough strain. Come help me get the tigers ready, since you're here. My father wants to practice for tomorrow's show."

"I didn't mean to add to your burden. I would never do that," he said quickly, raising his hand to tuck a curl behind her ear, then dropping his hand and looking away in sudden embarrassment. "I'm happy to help you. You know I listen to too many of auntie's stories. This one chore, I actually love. The tigers are beautiful, but fearsome."

Jasmine turned back to her task to hide the flush in her cheeks. "Remember that. They are dangerous, no matter how gorgeous. Wild animals are never fully tame," she said softly, putting the feed away and heading down the corridor toward the back courtyard that housed the tiger cages.

"No, you remember, Jasmine. Wild creatures are not to be trusted, especially Jinn!"

"Shhh. Do you want someone to hear you?" she whispered as they turned the corner and Ahmed opened the courtyard door.

The handlers and tiger trainers were already there when they arrived, grooming and caring for the beautiful beasts. They were huge, eight in all, the largest one well over five-hundred pounds. Though they were kept constantly clean and their straw freshly forked, there was no mistaking the animal scent permeating the warm courtyard. The group had been together for several years and chuffed and roared, communicating with one another, knowing their pack ranking, but like all wild animals testing their boundaries from time to time.

Jasmine went up to the head trainer. After greeting him with a warm smile, she said, "We intend to use all the tigers for the final act tomorrow, Rajah, so my father wants to practice it now. We'll be doing the swap as the finale, but he wants to do the levitation and appearance of all the tigers at once, with me floating in the air, center stage in place of Simba, above the revolving circles of fire."

"All at once? I'm not sure about that, Jasmine. How will we orchestrate that many cats? They aren't trained to stand stationary behind those little camouflage walls inside the cages for very long. The act would have to move pretty fast."

"Yes, we know. Don't worry. My father has it all under control. That's why we're going to do a practice drill today. Ahmed knows how it's supposed to be set up. He'll show you where the cages need to be. Can you help him get it ready while I go change my clothes?"

"Sure. We'll meet you on stage, Jasmine. If it works, it's going to be a great act."

"Oh, it'll work, and it's going to be a fantastic act," she agreed.

With a quick wave, Jasmine headed toward the service hallway and her rooms. She needed to be certain that Ornias, the Jinni of the Ring, was ready to perform his magic. Glancing down, she noticed that she was rubbing her thumb across the henna-hued tattoo on her wrist and dropped her hand to her side, hastening her departure. A movement in the hallway from the right caught her eye and she smiled. "Sheba," she said softly. "It won't be long now, my precious little familiar."

Reaching the elevator, she entered, slipped in her key card, hit the 4th floor button, and stepped back. The car moved up smoothly and silently, the doors swooshing open with a soft chime. She stepped out to the right until habit brought her to the third door where she used her pass key to enter her room. Sheba brushed against her leg to hurry past her, knowing her dinner was already waiting in the pantry.

Jasmine picked up the remote, downed the blinds, upped the lights, and locked the doors. She grabbed a bottle of water from the small fridge in the bar area, took a swig, and set it down. Her thumb found its way to the thin vertical scar on her wrist.

Ahmed had been helping her search for an artifact such as this ring for almost two years. Only a few magic-bearing items would have given her the potential magic she needed to boost her own power enough to escape the insidious financial and filial ties her uncle held over them.

Though they lived in the most likely place in all the world to find such a treasure, she still found it incredible that they recovered the most powerful talisman of all, *The Opal Ring* of King Solomon. She would have been willing to steal it to get away from Uncle Hassam.

Ahmed all but changed his mind right after they got back with their find. He nearly convinced her that they could find another way, some way that wouldn't land him on the bottom of the Nile in the belly of a crocodile. If it didn't work, she might still find herself chained in a brothel cell where her father couldn't find her and her uncle would. In the end, her personal desperation made her less terrified of the unknown consequences.

They spent another week researching the use and significances of the ring, and she prepared for its use, or so she assured Ahmed. Finally, casting a powerful protection spell within a guardian circle of salt, Ahmed at her side, she summoned the Jinni. He appeared as the ancient scrolls foretold, in a swirling pillar of fire. The Jinni acknowledged her as his mistress, too, the bearer of the ring, but he was so frightening, so obviously powerful.

Despite the protection spells she cast, Jasmine felt anxious with her new acquisition. This would be the second time she summoned the Jinni. She knew what to expect, she told herself. Taking a deep breath, Jasmine rubbed the ring on the middle finger of her right hand. The air around her crackled and sparked, a pillar of fire shot from floor to ceiling, swirling like a tornado, scorching hot, with pain but no damage, like hell, and in a puff of black smoke it disappeared. In its place stood an eight-foot Jinni, Ornias, once enslaved by King Solomon to carve stones for the building of the temple.

According to the mystic tomes, his enslavement was punishment for stealing gems from the royal treasury, gems he craved for their sparkling light. He would sink his vampire-like fangs into them and drain their glimmer in an effort to relieve the agony of eternal darkness—a life without the sun's blessing. This was the addiction Jasmine must feed in order to command the demonic Jinni's magic.

She concluded that his explosive manner of reappearance was certainly that of an escaping addict and it in no way reassured her. The Jinni was manlike in appearance, save that his skin was ebony not in an African ebony way, but more like a preternatural obsidian sheen with eyes that glowed golden like a cat's, but with a sunset luster that spoke of darker, more underground locales than mountaintops or beach horizons. "I hunger!" he bellowed.

Her own meager jewelry stash was nearly gone, so she spent every penny she had left to buy loose gemstones in the marketplace. She handed a few of those to him now. He snatched them eagerly. Next, if need be, she would take her uncle's ruby tie tack, with no remorse whatsoever—but she wouldn't involve Ahmed in even the knowing of it. It would be her sin and her consequences alone. On her terms.

The creature held a small stone in his hand. It grew to enormous proportions until she had to shield her eyes from the luster of its gleam. He smiled, a hideous distortion of happiness, and his incisors distended, enabling him to sink his teeth into the magically engorged gems.

She watched in amazement as he appeared to suck the stone's shine until the blue topaz turned first gray and then black as coal. He repeated the process with first the small garnet and then the sapphire she had given him. Then, sated for the moment, he said, "Your wishes, mistress?"

"I wish to be protected, from my uncle. I also wish to have you aid my father's magic." She went on to explain the details of her plan.

***

The audience went silent as the eight cages rose in the air. They hovered, shoulder-height to The Amazing Ben Ali as he stood center stage, arms raised. He walked to the cage closest to him and with a quick tug pulled the gold drape from the previously empty cage, revealing a full grown Bengal tiger. As if on cue, it roared to the accompanying gasps and ah's of the appreciative audience.

Ben Ali hurried from cage to cage, releasing the drapery and revealing six more Bengal tigers. But when he came to the center cage, the one that had in fact already contained a tiger, what he revealed instead was Jasmine, smiling and waving. The cages slowly lowered to the floor, and The Amazing Ben Ali opened the cage to release Jasmine, who he led to center stage where they took a bow and turned to gesture toward the tigers.

When they stepped forward, the curtain came down behind them, allowing the handlers to hurry the tigers off stage and away from the wild applause that made the cats nervous and skittish, back to their larger cages, juicy meat treats and quiet praise from familiar voices. Jasmine bent her head one last time, gestured toward the true star, her father, and then graciously backed away, smiling with joy at her father's beaming pride.

The talent scout was waiting for them backstage once her father finished his second curtain call. He laughed when her father just shrugged and refused to divulge the levitation method used for the cages. The scout, a self-proclaimed amateur magician himself, was unable to find the wires. Despite his disappointment, the man produced the coveted contract, and Jasmine managed to keep from squealing with excitement as she hurried off to find Ahmed and allow her father to finish his business negotiations.

Once in the corridor, she noticed a burning sensation on the middle finger of her right hand. Looking down, she saw that the pentagram on the opal ring glowed from within. It pulsed with radiant fire, sparks of blue and green, orange and gold twinkled up and down the lines of the symbol.

She felt Sheba brushing against her legs, swishing her tail and winding in and out around her ankles as if she could feel the electrical impulses the ring generated. The burning sensation increased and the gold began to glow with a rosy hue, almost molten. Jasmine grabbed hold of the ring and tried to pull it from her finger, but it wouldn't budge. Rushing into a nearby restroom, she turned on a faucet and plunged her hand under the cool water. It had no effect.

She rubbed against the ring, trying to ease it off her finger, and in so doing activated the stone. The room vibrated and a pillar of fire erupted from the floor to ceiling, then exploded into a puff of smoke and the Jinni appeared.

The ring immediately stopped burning and returned to its natural state. "You did that! What are you doing?" Jasmine demanded.

"I hunger!" declared the Jinni, clearly agitated.

"But I fed you just before the performance and I don't have any more gemstones right now. I told you I will get you more tomorrow. You said ruby and diamonds last the longest and I will get you some from my evil uncle tomorrow. I know where he keeps them. My father got his contract and everything is going to be okay now."

"I hunger!" shouted the Jinni.

"Okay, okay." Jasmine pushed air with her hands, indicated that he should be quiet. She bent down and was surprised and relieved to see no one was in the bathroom. "I will get them now. He will be in the club for a few more hours, so no one will be in his rooms. Get back in the ring and I will get them for you now."

"As you command, mistress," the Jinni said, and vanished.

Jasmine took a deep breath. Glancing in the mirror, she noted the smudged knoll under her left eye and wet a paper hand towel to wipe at the smear. Then, splashing a bit of cool water on each flushed cheek, she dabbed them dry, dropped the towel in the trash can and pulled the door open, nearly colliding with a middle-aged tourist in a sequined gown, chatting into an International iPhone. Murmuring an apology, she turned right and hurried to the elevator.

By the time the elevator reached the 7th floor, she managed to get her breathing back to normal. As the door swept open, she stepped out and looked toward the end of the corridor, where her uncle occupied the last two rooms. He converted them into one oversized suite, reserving the penthouse suites on the upper floors for up-charged guests. A few less gems were certainly not going to hurt him, and he'd been underpaying her and her father for six years. As if the fact that he'd been molesting her since she was a twelve-year-old child didn't deserve payback. He had whatever she did coming to him, and then some, she reasoned.

Not that she had any choice, she reminded herself, as she paused at the storage room door and slid her pass key through the card reader. She stepped inside, found a box of latex gloves and wriggled her fingers into a pair, then hurried back into the hallway.

Soon she was swallowing her fear as she approached his door. Knocking, and then holding her breath in case he should actually be in for some bizarre twist of fate, Jasmine glanced back down the corridor. When no one responded, she pulled out the pass key she'd had forever, and shoved it in the card reader. The lights flashed green from left to right and back again. She heard the familiar click and pressed down on the lever. The door opened, and she was in. Just like that.

Looking around, she was surprised at the décor in her uncle's suite. She wasn't sure what she expected, but it was nothing like hers or her father's rooms, and nothing like the plush lobby or even the elegantly appointed dining room, casino or showroom where her father and some Arabian dancing girls performed. It was beautiful, but it was modern and designed with western European furnishings.

She could have been standing in the lobby of a New York City loft on the Upper East Side, not the entrance to a Cairo hotel owner's suite. Where were the gilded ankhs and busts of Pharaohs and framed papyrus fragments? Surely, he should have at least one statue of Isis or an Eye of Horus for good luck? He was such a hypocrite. The man did nothing but put her down for being an uppity American and yet he surrounded himself with Western everything.

Jasmine laughed at the irony but had no time to wonder what further perversions her twisted uncle harbored. She hurried in the direction she felt would be his bedroom and sought out the closet. How convenient of her uncle to use the same architect and designer for all the family suites. Though much grander than her small suite, the closet was similar. He was so predictable in some ways.

Finding the remote, she picked it up right where he left it, on top of his dresser in the middle of his closet. Jasmine pressed the button that opened his drawers. She found his jewel valet easily enough too, in the same general location as her own meager and now nearly empty small-cubby-partitioned drawer. Upon discovering far more gems than expected, she helped herself to a pair of diamond cufflinks as well as the large ruby tie tack she had seen him wear on several occasions, closed the drawers and ran toward the entry door.

She was out the door and waiting for the elevator before it dawned on her that she had just committed a burglary. In fact, she was now a jewel thief, a cat burglar. Perhaps she should teach Sheba to burgle. The Jinni would have to make the security camera footage glitch her out of the appropriate time frames of course, and the pass card key code would have to be erased from the system on her uncle's door, but other than the electronic help from the Jinni it had gone much easier than she could have wished.

An elderly couple exited the elevator, barely noticing her as she stepped inside and pushed the 4th floor button. What was one more Arabian dancing girl in Cairo? She had to get out of her costume. Remembering her gloves, she pulled them off and wadded them into a ball in her hand. The door chimed and she exited, thankful that no one was waiting to enter. She hurried to her rooms, shoved her key card into the reader and all but slammed it behind her, collapsing against it. Shaking, reaction catching up to her, she reached down to scoop up Sheba whose immediate response to her traumatic entrance served to soothe her.

"Aw," she said softly, responding to the gentle purr and rubbing of the round head against her neck that her spiritual familiar offered by way of a tender snuggle. "Thanks, Sheba. I needed that."

Setting Sheba on the floor, she picked up the gloves and tossed them in the trash. She knew what had to be done. Jasmine rubbed the ring and watched as the Jinni appeared, eager to see what she brought him. His golden eyes sparkled when he saw that she had a ruby as well as twin diamonds.

"You have done very well indeed, mistress. Ornias is grateful."

"Good. I need you to erase my image from the hotel video cameras and my hotel pass key code from my uncle's room card reader so they can't connect me with the disappearance of these gems. I probably should have told you that before I did it, but I'm not exactly a professional."

The Jinni waved his hand in a casual manner and said, "It is done, mistress. A small matter."

"What spell did you use?" Jasmine asked, curiosity making her bold.

Ornias paused. He lowered the already enlarged ruby and bent forward to gaze at her intently. Grabbing her wrist, he turned it over and held it within his hand and studied the henna-hued likeness of Sheba, the sun-rendered pentagram, the little kitty paw prints, and then looked again, deep into her eyes, her soul, and said, "So, you are a witch who wishes to be a sorceress, it would seem. Why did you not just voice this wish aloud, mistress?"

"I-I. No one knows of this. I have never..."

"But I, Ornias, most powerful of all magic casters should have sensed this flicker of power secreted away within you, mistress. I was too consumed by my own addictions to notice what lurks in the hearts of those around me. I have been too long in solitude it would seem."

Suddenly he shrank, becoming a mere six foot tall with mocha human skin tone, and strode over to Jasmine's closet, throwing open the door. He walked to the back and stood before her altar, observing her statue of Isis, her incense burner, her chest of herbs and apothecary spices and resins.

"Upon King Solomon's death, I bound myself to this ring and hid it where I felt no one would ever find it. What I should have done is destroy it, this ring that had for so many years controlled me. I thought if I left this world, I would no longer suffer. Little did I realize that my hunger would only grow as I languished in this void, a prisoner of my own foolish whim. I see now that I must break my own spell."

He rummaged through her chest, pulling out what he sought, grinding some ingredients using her mortar and pestle. When he was done, he put out his hand and said, "The ring."

She hesitated, but didn't dare defy him, so handed him the ring. After all, he had already granted her wishes. The coming true part was under way, and she had paid the fee.

He placed the ring upon the altar, gestured toward it and it sparked and flamed. A softly chanted incantation in an ancient tongue she didn't recognize filled the small confines of her closet and the flickering flames from the fire cast strange shadows upon the walls. It made her imagine she saw dancing creatures, bathed in flames, horns protruding from their foreheads. But in an instant they were gone. The flame snuffed itself out. The incantation over, the Jinni said, "Here, a pretty bauble now, but my prison no more," and handed her the ring.

She took it and slipped it back on her finger, silently, not sure what, if anything she should say. A knock on the door saved her the decision. The Jinni disappeared, as if in agreement. Confused, Jasmine looked around her closet, which was now once again as she always kept it, the way her mother taught her. She went into her bedroom and closed the door behind her, then went into the foyer to answer her door.

The peep hole revealed Ahmed, much to her relief, and she quickly opened the door.

"I heard you have good news for me!"

"If you already heard, it's not news," she said.

"I thought you'd be happier," he said, head tilted, studying her. "What's wrong?"

"Nothing."

"Ha! If there's one thing I've learned in life it's that whenever a female says that, the opposite is true. I have five sisters, remember? Give!"

Jasmine laughed without humor. "Okay. The Jinni broke the spell and is no longer tied to the ring. I am no longer his mistress, but it doesn't matter because as you already know I was granted my wishes."

"Ah, is that all? Well, that's more good news if you ask me. That means we are now free of him. I was very worried. No good can ever come of messing with a Jinni. They are dangerous. Even if you have them under a spell, unlike angels they have free will and so can be very, very evil and are powerful sorcerers, unrivaled in their casting of spells and curses."

"And just how do you know all this?" Jasmine demanded.

"My auntie was telling me the legend of--"

"Not more of your auntie's stories now, Ahmed. Come on. I have to shower and change. And I'm starving. How about I meet you for dinner in an hour so we can celebrate my father's new contract. I'm sure he has already gone out with the talent scout and his magician friends. We can go to the café in the square that you like so much. It's open late tonight."

"A plan I can work with. It'll give me time to go change. I didn't know we were going out. I will be downstairs in the lobby in one hour." With a quick wave, Ahmed was out the door.

***

Jasmine reached up to touch her talisman, and stopped. Going back to her bathroom, she scanned the countertop, then retraced her route to her closet and looked through her jewelry valet but couldn't find her necklace anywhere.

She knew she wore it during tonight's performance. She always said a small protection spell her mother taught her before going on stage.

The cage. There had been a slight tug on her neck as she slipped into the hidden compartment in the bottom of the tiger cage. The necklace must have fallen off. Perhaps she snagged it on something and broke the clasp. It was a cherished gift from her mother. She had to find it. Grabbing her key card, Jasmine headed for the door. Ahmed wouldn't be waiting yet as she was ready twenty minutes early.

The elevator opened as soon as she pushed the button. It then swooped straight to the ground floor. She quickly went to the big room off the courtyard where they housed the tigers and equipment overnight and let herself in with her key card. The cats, already settled for the evening, stirred at the unexpected intruder, but settled down once she spoke to them quietly. Hers was a familiar, calming voice.

She approached the stage cages and found the one with the markings she sought. Opening the door with a soft clanking noise, she stepped inside and lifted the trap door in the floor.

"Hey, little mouse. I saw you come in here. Come to play with the big kitties?"

She froze. Her uncle. He followed her. Quietly, she lowered herself into the small cubicle and closed the door, concealing herself as she had done so many times before. As she lowered her hand, it fell upon a cluster of stones. Her necklace. She clasped it tightly, repeating the protection spell in her head, over and over.

"Come out, come out, wherever you are, little mouse. There's only one way out."

His voice was close now. He sounded like he was right outside the cage. She closed her eyes and squeezed the talisman, wishing their positions were reversed.

Suddenly, she was standing outside the cage.

"Hey, what the hell just happened? Where am I?" shouted her uncle.

Pounding sounded on the underside of the trap door of the cage.

"Let me out of here!"

Jasmine stared, fascinated that her wish came true. But then a Bengal tiger appeared in the cage, and then another. They roared, and it was a hungry sounding roar. Very hungry.

The trap door popped open.

Jasmine stared, transfixed in horrified fascination as her uncle's shouts of outrage became screams of agony until there was silence except for the rending and chomping and crunching and gnawing and slurping. And the gasping, of course, there was gasping and panting, but that was Jasmine, not the tigers. She was half-way to hyperventilating when the Jinni appeared.

"Let your breath out slowly. Would you like a paper bag?"

She shook her head and forced air from her lungs, then more air, then a little more. Then she allowed a bit to come back in. Then out. Her hands were clutching her throat and she loosened them. Once she could speak, she said, "I didn't wish this. Never this. Why couldn't my own magic have just worked?"

"Your own magic? But it did. Why do you think he never raped and tortured you, like the other girls in the hotel?"

"But he molested me!"

"Yes, he was a monster. And he did so much worse to so many. His fate is as it should be, but you had to be toughened up to fit the role for which you have been chosen. You are not asking the right questions."

"What? What role have I been chosen for? What questions should I ask?"

"You are not asking why King Solomon was given dominion over me."

"But I thought it was because you stole gems."

"Do you think for this reason alone the Archangel Michael would be sent to give King Solomon the means to control me?"

Jasmine gasped. It was a reasonable explanation, but when put like that, it did seem as though the crime may not fit the punishment. "Wh-what did you do?"

"I do not have these," he opened his mouth and displayed his fearsome incisors, causing her to back away a step, "just so that I can suck the light from gemstones." He appeared inside the cage. The tigers were now gone. Grasping what was left of her uncle, he drew him up and again opened his mouth. Sparks, blue, green, orange, yellow and purple twinkled along two continuous threads of cosmic plasma that pulsed from her uncle's corpse through the straw-like suction of the Jinni's teeth into the Jinni's essence. She knew this because once again his skin was translucent obsidian in appearance and she could see the same cosmic sparking burst throughout his being like a galaxy creation. Her uncle was pulp, puff, gone.

"S-soul sucker," Jasmine whispered, eyes wide with shock, body shaking like a forgotten thread yet to be woven into the tapestry of life.

"Very astute."

"What do you want of me?" she asked, dreading the answer.

"What I was promised," the Jinni said. "What your mother promised and failed to deliver," he added. Then he vanished.

"My mother?"

She spun around, but the room was truly empty. Running to the door, she flung it open and ran to the elevator. A young man collided with her when the doors opened. He apologized, though it was clearly her fault. Jasmine nodded, distracted, and pushed the 4th floor button.

Her father was probably out, but she had to be sure. The elevator took forever, stopping at every floor to let guests on or off. Tempering her impatience with difficulty, she finally got off and hurried to her father's rooms.

A knock on his door was answered almost immediately by a, "Come on in, I'm on the phone."

Thrilled to hear her father's voice, Jasmine hurried inside just as her father said, "Thanks, medium rare is perfect," and hung up.

"You didn't go out with the talent scout or your friends? Did something go wrong?" she asked, suddenly concerned about her father's contract deal, wondering if the Jinni had done something.

"He had to catch a flight, and I had a slight headache, so made arrangements to celebrate with them tomorrow night. It's been a long weekend. The contract is all signed, sealed, and filed with my attorney, so no worries there, my dear."

"Oh, good, about the contract. Congratulations, father. I knew you would get the deal. I'm sorry you're not feeling well though."

"Just a slight headache. Nothing at all, really. Took some aspirin and it's already on its way out."

"Great. How soon do we leave for America?" Not soon enough for her. She wanted to get away from Egypt and the Jinni immediately. How long before they went looking for her uncle? He was such a pervert he sometimes disappeared for a few days at a time to some hellhole brothel, probably where he could do things depraved and illegal to underage street children no one ever missed. Cairo had enough of them, unfortunately.

The Jinni was probably right about that. Considering what her uncle was capable of, her magic probably had saved her from some even nastier horrors. But she had an unsettling suspicion that somehow the Jinni or those who served him allowed her uncle to abuse her in order to, how had he put it, toughen her up. Jasmine shuddered. It would be great if they could be gone before he was missed.

"Are you cold?"

"What? Oh, no. Just had a chill. Ever felt like someone walked over your grave type of thing?" Jasmine wrapped her arms around herself and rubbed her upper arms to dispel the goose flesh.

Her father's eyes transfixed with horror as he stared at her right hand. He reached out and pointed with his index finger.

"What is it?" she asked.

"That ring! Where did you get it?"

"This?" She grasped the opal ring and began to tug on it, twisting and turning, but it refused to move.

Her father grabbed her hand and pulled it until she finally cried out in protest. "We have to get it off," he said. "How did you find it? I flushed it down the commode on the jet before we landed six years ago!"

"What? What are you saying, father? You have seen this ring before?"

He backed away and ran his hand through his hair, looking haggard, older than his forty-eight years. "It was your mother's. It was buried with her."

"Then how could you have had it on the plane? You're not making sense." *Her mother's? Had her mother been the Jinni's last mistress?*

"You were too old for dolls, but you kept it with you because your mother had given it to you. I opened the window blind on the plane and the sunlight sparkled off the opal on the ring. It was around the doll's ponytail."

"So how do you know mother didn't put it there on the doll?"

"She couldn't do it anymore, couldn't stand being around those vile men, and couldn't see what that creature did to them. She tried to explain, tried to bargain with the Jinni, but he wouldn't see reason. We were going to flee, find someone who could break the spell, but the very next day that car, it came out of nowhere." He wasn't focused on Jasmine any more, but seemed to be reliving the incident in his mind, the terror of it fresh on his face. "Do you really think it was just an accident?"

"What?" *Her beautiful, sweet mother had fed the Jinni souls? Sinful souls like her uncle's?* "The Jinni killed momma?"

"She just couldn't make herself available to all those hideous, evil perverts any more, the kind of dark souls the Jinni savors. She would never have led the Jinni to her own beloved daughter. I saw the ring on her finger when I closed her casket myself!" He staggered back, clutching at his chest.

"Father!" Jasmine rushed forward, grabbing his arm. "What is it?"

"Just out of breath. Nothing," he said, gasping. But then his knees buckled, and he fell to the floor, doubled over in pain.

Jasmine grabbed the phone and called the front desk, demanding the house doctor and an ambulance. She hurried back to her father, whose face was blue, eyes open but staring straight ahead, and loosened his collar. "Father, can you hear me?"

The air crackled and a pillar of fire erupted from floor to ceiling, exploded into a swirl of smoke and the Jinni appeared and said, "He doesn't look too good, does he?"

"Can you do something?" Jasmine sobbed.

"Can or will? Do you wish I would?" inquired the Jinni, sounding almost sympathetic. "I'm really very hungry though," he added.

A knock sounded on the door and Jasmine yelled, "Come in, hurry!"

Ahmed raced into the room. "What's wrong? I heard the front desk call for a doctor and ambulance for your father's room!"

"Very," said the Jinni again. "He looks tasty."

Ahmed stopped. He looked at the Jinni, then back at Jasmine, crouched on the floor next to her father. "No. Wait! I'll get someone," he said, running from the room. A moment later, he was back, dragging the room service attendant with her father's dinner cart. "Look. Will he do?"

Jasmine stared at Omar, recalled him hiding behind the floor-to-ceiling drapes of an empty hotel suite, peering out while her uncle fondled and punished her naked flesh with blows that left bruises in both hidden and permanent places. The look on his face had not been sympathy, though the words he had expressed later were all the right ones, fearing retribution should her uncle discover his witness of the incestuous incident. Even so, could she hand his soul over to this demon, become every bit as monstrous as the Jinni himself? She looked down at her father, then back at Omar, who fixated on the Jinni in mute dread.

"Yes, why not him?" Jasmine said softly.

"Why not indeed," said the Jinni. With a wave of Ornias' hand, the young service attendant wreathed on the floor, clutching his chest. Within moments the heaving of his chest slowed and then stopped. The Jinni approached. He reached down to grasp the young man's shirt front and lifted him from the carpet. When he opened his mouth, his incisors extended, and the cosmic feeding frenzy Jasmine had previously witnessed was played out for Ahmed's horrified edification.

The service attendant disappeared within the Jinni, who also vanished, and then Jasmine's father stirred and looked around. Sitting up, he said, "What happened?"

Indeed, thought Jasmine with a shudder, tears running unchecked down her face. She exchanged a bewildered look with Ahmed and said, "You passed out, father. The doctor and paramedics are on the way. I fear you may have had a stroke, or a heart episode of some kind."

"What? I'm too young for such things, surely. Funny I don't seem to recall anything past signing that contract this evening. There now, what's this? Don't cry, my little angel. I'm fine."

"You remember nothing?" Jasmine asked.

"No. Wait, is that my supper? I remember ordering supper. Starving too."

A knock sounded. "Finally. Come in!" Jasmine called out, wiping at her face and reaching for the tissue Ahmed held out to her. The doctor, followed closely by the paramedics with a stretcher arrived.

"I'm so sorry. I wasn't on the premises. Came back as soon as I got the call. What seems to be the problem?" the doctor asked.

Jasmine rose to her feet. "My father. He complained of a headache earlier. Then he had chest pains, passed out, turned blue, and he wasn't breathing well. He took aspirin. Seems better now, but he doesn't remember any of it, which worries me too," she said quickly before her father could tell the doctor nothing was wrong with him.

"Let's take a look," the doctor said, taking the stethoscope from his neck, putting the ends in his ears and placing it on her father's chest despite his protests. He placed his fingertips against her father's wrist and monitored his watch. Satisfied, he nodded and said. "We're going to take you in and run a couple tests. Best to be safe." Her father started to complain and the doctor added, "For your daughter's sake," which gained his begrudging cooperation.

"We'll be right behind you, father."

"Yes, not to worry. I will accompany Jasmine so the doctor may ride with you to hospital," Ahmed said.

"Thank you," Jasmine said. "I need to run to my room and get my purse. Then we'll be right behind you."

They waited until the paramedics loaded her father onto the gurney and wheeled him into the hallway before rushing down the hall to Jasmine's room.

When they entered, she pushed the on lights button and rushed into the living room.

"He'll be fine, you know."

"Ah!" she cried out, jumping, startled to find the Jinni seated casually waiting for her.

"You got what you wanted," Ahmed said, stepping in front of her, protectively, though she could see his hands shaking and hear the tremor in his voice. "Why are you here?"

"They will tell you he has had a mild stroke, the only side effect of which will be the memory loss. I'm afraid he won't remember the secrets you wish to know of his time with your mother either, though I'll not rob him of their love. That would be needlessly cruel. Don't you agree?"

"You have become one of the monsters you feast upon," Jasmine said softly. Then, more forcefully, "Did you kill my mother? Did you trick me into finding the ring?"

"What?" Ahmed said. "I thought your mother died in an auto accident, and I found the ring in that shop."

"So did I, until my father told me just now that the Jinni killed her, and that this ring belonged to her, first. Just how did it come to be there, in plain sight, just when you were at the antique store looking, and how did that dealer not know it for what it was?" Jasmine insisted.

"Your mother broke her end of the bargain," the Jinni said, smiling without amusement. "But what of you, Ahmed? And you, Jasmine? You both were so eager to sacrifice another to take your place. What does that make you?"

"My motives were selfish enough," admitted, Ahmed. "I thought to protect Jasmine."

A familiar static brushed against Jasmine's leg and she glanced down to see Sheba butting her head against her leg, demanding attention.

"Who would protect her from you if I were gone? And Omar was no innocent. I had yet to prove it, but I know he was providing her uncle with young, underage girls. We've had him under surveillance for other reasons, too."

"Not now, Sheba," Jasmine said softly, then supporting Ahmed's claims she added, "I knew he was a twisted bastard all along."

"Very tasty," confirmed the Jinni. "Does it make you feel better about his demise?"

"No!" They both echoed.

"But don't you see, you would do the world a favor as well as yourselves. You will wed. A little white chapel perhaps? Together you shall sate my hunger. You will find vile and depraved souls for my feasting. Vegas is the perfect banquet hall for one such as me."

"What? We aren't even engaged." Jasmine said. "Ouch." She brushed Sheba away with her foot, annoyed that her beloved familiar had actually sunk her teeth into her ankle.

"You will be. Soon. Ahmed has loved you for a long time. Surely you know this. Tell her, Ahmed."

"This is not the time or place for such talk, and it's none of your business," Ahmed said, frowning. "What happened? Did Sheba bite you?" He reached toward the Siamese who instantly hissed and arched her back, striking out at him with her claw.

"Sheba! What has gotten into you?" Jasmine reached down and picked the cat up, snugging her against herself and the cat seemed to settle down.

"You are evading my questions, Jinni," Jasmine said, turning her attention back to their current problem with her usual focus.

"Your mother and father made a bargain that they didn't keep. They wanted a child and would do anything to have it. I kept my end of the bargain. You are that child, Jasmine. And now you will fulfil their end of the bargain."

"Their end of the bargain? What did they owe you?"

"You know."

He was right. She knew. She knew the Jinni's true addiction was dark, evil souls to feast upon. In her mindless desire to escape her uncle's clutches she had thought any price worth paying. Ahmed's cautions and begging for her to change her mind had fallen on deaf ears. Instead, she dragged him, knowing all along how much he loved her, into the Jinni's evil clutches, despite her good intentions. Jasmine looked at the opal ring and tried to pull it from her finger, but just as she had known all along it was there to stay.

Ahmed had been right. Jinn lied. She looked into his eyes, tears of regret running down her face. He reached to tenderly wipe at them with a tissue. Then handed it to her, before pulling her close and letting her duck her head against his chest to cry.

Sheba let out a growl and hiss. Jasmine glanced up. Angled against him, she chanced to see what looked like gratitude pass from Ahmed to the Jinni. Then Ahmed rested his cheek upon the top of her head and snuggled her. But what once would seem gentle now seemed possessive.

She closed her eyes, blinded by tears, seeing more clearly at last with her third eye. The Jinni had enchanted the ring to enslave her, like her mother before her. Had he used her father to trap her mother as he was using Ahmed now? Was that the real reason her father drank?

A shudder caused her shoulders to tremble. Ahmed rubbed her back. It didn't comfort her. It sent chills up her spine.

Sheba hissed.

Her uncle was a practice run. She was to endure the constant company of men so depraved and lecherous they wanted to perform illegal and bestial acts upon either her or whatever helpless victims they thought she would provide. Night after night she would be expected to lure perverts into the hands of a dark soul sucking Jinni.

Perhaps Ahmed really believed he would be happy protecting her from men like that so that their baser desires were left unfulfilled until the Jinni's were met. But did he believe she could respect a man who would wish this life for her?

She felt Sheba's gentle connection as the cat rubbed her head against her neck and wondered what further secrets her psychic familiar was trying to reveal to her. Was it true what they said about the spirits of the dead returning in the form of sacred cats? The feline purred loudly. Fine hairs along her neck rose.

"Get busy!"

Jasmine jumped, startled by the booming command.

"Cast your spells and entice your beasts, young sorceress. And keep her safe, Ahmed. I hunger!"

Rubbing her check against Sheba's velvety fur, she whispered, "I'm listening, mama. We will defeat them all."

Somehow.

Elizabeth Alsobrooks

Since retiring from her "day" jobs, Elizabeth lives with her personal social media editor, Tashi (AKA Lhasa Apso), and husband, Kenton, (AKA Irish-Scotsman) at the foot of the beautiful Santa Catalina Mountain Range in the Grand Canyon state of AZ. She loves to hike or sit on her patio sipping coffee (or wine) and reading or brainstorming plots and enjoys the grandeur of her mountain views.

These days, she divides her writing time between urban fantasy, horror, and nonfiction. Work on her Illuminati series continues, but she loves throwing out a horror short on occasion. She grew up with a love for Shakespeare, Chaucer, Poe, Dickens, the Bronte sisters and Koontz, so her taste is as eclectic as her range. That creative range reaches to oil painting and sculpting, as well as learning to play the piano, now that she has time to pursue more interests she always loved.

Rob Tucker

Author and retired business and management consultant in a wide range of industries throughout the country, Rob resides with his wife in Southern California.

He is a graduate of the University of California, Santa Barbara and of the University of California, Los Angeles with Bachelor's and Master's of Fine Arts Degrees. He is a recipient of the Samuel Goldwyn and Donald Davis Literary Awards and has also worked in advertising, corporate communications, and media production.

An affinity for family and generations pervades his novels.

His works are literary and genre fiction that address the nature and importance of personal integrity

Ric Wasley

Ric has a 40-year professional career history in advertising, publishing, and marketing in Boston, New York and San Francisco. He has degrees in history and psychology and has been trained in debating, public speaking and stage acting. A large part of his 40-year career was spent in numerous professional and business settings as a presenter and featured speaker at seminars and professional meetings.

Ric has been a visiting professor at Worcester Polytech Institute. He also teaches a popular course on marketing for authors at prominent venues such as the venerable "Cape Cod Writers Conference". Ric is a published author of a Mystery Series and multiple other novels.

Darren Simon

Darren Simon has been a writer for much of his life. His career has included working as a journalist in Los Angeles, Israel and Southern California along the Mexican and Arizona borders. He presently works in government affairs on California water issues, teaches college English for the California Community College system, and does freelance writing for regional magazines.

His work as an author focuses on middle grade and young adult readers to inspire them to read the way he was inspired, first by comic books and then the science fiction and fantasy novels that were so important to his youth. He resides in California's Desert Southwest with his wife and sons.

Sean Brink

Shawn D. Brink resides in Eastern Nebraska and has been writing since old enough to hold a pencil. He is currently building a following with four novels to his name. His fifth novel, *Pets for Legion*, will be published through Tell-Tale Publishing in the near future. Shawn also has numerous shorter works in various publications and anthologies. When not writing, he spends time with family, and enjoys playing guitar.

Shawn is represented by Liverman Literary Agency.

Francesca Quarto

Francesca is part of a large Italian family where she discovered early on that a love of reading was as much a part of her DNA as her mother's skill at baking. Growing up in a house filled with laughter, screaming, banging pots, fighting and loving family bonds, shaped her life and heart.

Having moved from the east coast where she was raised between New York and New Jersey, Francesca left for the mid-west where she spent several years outside the Chicago area raising a family of three children, completing her college degrees and writing introspective poetry like other young mothers.

Francesca has worked in local television, a small city zoo, founded a non-profit tutoring agency for an inner-city neighborhood which eventually served local school districts, worked for an International Evangelical Television and Radio Station and for a non-profit organization serving challenged adults.

Francesca Quarto resides in a small town outside Indianapolis, Indiana with her husband Patrick. She still has a great love of the written word and while she enjoys her E-Reader immensely, she still treasures the excitement of turning the next page.

Tell-Tale would like to thank you for your purchase. If you would like to read more by these or other fine TT authors, please visit our website:

www.tell-talepublishing.com

www.ingramcontent.com/pod-product-compliance
Lightning Source LLC
Chambersburg PA
CBHW030636190726
48286CB00008B/2539